CW00546832

**Science fiction magazine from Scotland**

ISSN 2059-2590

Shoreline of Infinity is available in digital or print editions.
Submissions of fiction, art, reviews, poetry, non-fiction are welcomed:
visit the website to find out how to submit.
www.shorelineofinfinity.com
Publisher
The New Curiosity Shop
Edinburgh
Scotland
100916

# Contents

Pull up a Log . . . . . . . . . . . . . . . . . . . . . .3

The Revolution Will Be Catered . . . . . .5
Iain Maloney

Neme . . . . . . . . . . . . . . . . . . . . . . . . . . .15
Jack Schouten

What Goes Up . . . . . . . . . . . . . . . . . . . .25
Stuart Beel

Possible Side Effects . . . . . . . . . . . . . . .29
Adam Connors

Nothing to Fear. . . . . . . . . . . . . . . . . . .41
Nat Newman

Perennials. . . . . . . . . . . . . . . . . . . . . . . .45
Daniel Rosen

Incoming . . . . . . . . . . . . . . . . . . . . . . . .59
Thomas Clark

Overkill. . . . . . . . . . . . . . . . . . . . . . . . . .67
Rob Butler

When There is no Sun . . . . . . . . . . . . . .71
Craig Thomson

SF Caledonia . . . . . . . . . . . . . . . . . . . . .90
Monica Burns

Phantastes . . . . . . . . . . . . . . . . . . . . . . .96
George MacDonald

Interview: Simon Morden . . . . . . . . 106

Noise and Sparks 2:
You Have to Live. . . . . . . . . . . . . . . . 114
Ruth EJ Booth

Reviews. . . . . . . . . . . . . . . . . . . . . . . . 118

Multiverse . . . . . . . . . . . . . . . . . . . . . 127
Russell Jones
Andrew Blair          129
Ruth Aylett            130

Parabolic Puzzles . . . . . . . . . . . . . . . 132
Paul Holmes

**Cover:** Sara Julia

## Editorial Team
*Editor-in-Chief:*
Noel Chidwick

*Art Director:*
Mark Toner

*Deputy Editor/Poetry Editor:*
Russell Jones

*Reviews Editor:*
Iain Maloney

*Assistant Editor & First Reader:*
Monica Burns

**With thanks to Emily Walsh, Rosie Gailor, Anna Williamson and Sean Larney**

## First Contact

*Web:*
www.shorelineofinfinity.com
*Email:*
contact@shorelineofInfinity.com
*Twitter:* @shoreinf
and on Facebook

# Pull up a Log

**By now you will have witnessed** the hideous reveal in the fourth of our series of covers by artist Sara Julia. Originally from Switzerland, Sara is a comic artist and illustrator based in Edinburgh and she has been on the Shoreline art team since issue one in which she provided the artwork for *Approaching 43,000 Candles* (Guy T Martland)—a story that I thought well nigh impossible to illustrate. Well done Sara for proving me wrong.

By issue 2 we decided to give Sara the cover and she produced a wonderful seasonal scene from the Shoreline of Infinity world with a mysterious figure enjoying the view. We were so impressed by this that we wondered how she would approach the other three seasons and offered her a series of covers culminating in the one in this volume, and now you can follow a year in the life of the strange space explorer.

Here is a little idea for budding Shoreline writers. Our editorial team might be very interested in a well-written story filling out Sara's cover illustrations. Just saying.

This has proved such a good concept that we are starting into a new series of four covers by Sara's fellow Shoreline artist Stephen Pickering. Long ago, Stephen moved from England to Scotland's wild south west and he brings a lovely old school aesthetic to our pages. He also started with us in issue one illustrating *See You Later* (M Luke McDonell) and providing the sequence of images for our story competition. So watch the next four covers to see the adventures of Stephen's character, The Reader, and future issues for more sequenced art stories from the worlds that meet on the Shoreline of Infinity.

*Mark Toner*
*Art Director*
*Shoreline of Infinity*
*September 2016*

# The Revolution Will Be Catered

## Iain Maloney

Art: P Emerson Williams

"**W**ake up, Zeke. Wake up."

Zeke coughed, a hacking, rattling expulsion that shook him alert. He leaned over the side of his bed and spat into the cereal bowl. Something with more filaments than saliva should consist of splattered into the previous night's dribble of milk and flakes. He pulled himself up onto his knees, his head still buried in the pillow.

"Wake up, Zeke. This is your wake-up call. It's 00:00. Wake up."

"I'm ... uh ... up."

In the darkness, he found the drinking tube and yanked it towards him, letting the cool, filtered water wash away the taste coating his mouth. He coughed again, spat again, then arched his back, stretching and cracking the sleep out of his bones.

It was still dark outside. He shifted through a few basic yoga positions, his blood belatedly beginning to flow. It was still dark outside—the thought was insistent. Living on the forty-seventh floor Zeke rarely bothered tinting the windows. So a few birds occasionally caught sight of him naked, and even if the window-cleaning bots sometimes surprised him, it wasn't worth the effort of giving the command to the House each morning and night. He and the House got along best if they left each other alone.

Dark?

"House, what time did you say it was?"

"It is now 00:09."

"You woke me at midnight?"

"Correct."

"Why?"

"So that you would be awake."

"Logic? That's what you offer me?" His alarm was set for 08:50 every day so he could sign on with work at 09:00, as per his terms and conditions. "Why would I need to be awake nine hours before work?"

"You do not have work today."

"What?" Zeke hadn't had a day off in six years. With the House connected to the work network, and the implants and the software upgrades they'd installed in his creative cortex, he could continue to work twenty-four seven. Thankfully, the unions had negotiated that down to twelve on, twelve off. Technically, his cortex was always working, mulling over ideas, extracting details from his dreams and memories, turning it all into raw data from which he could work when awake and signed in. Still, even the unions had to agree that it couldn't really be classified as work if you were fast asleep at the time. But a day off? You weren't even allowed those on compassionate grounds these days, not since the whole world was finally networked. You could still be productive from a church pew.

Zeke wandered through to the living room, where his work station stood ready for his input. Bots had cleaned during the night, and the mess of pizza and vodka shots he'd left had disappeared. He'd spent the evening gaming with Victor up on fifty-nine and Inira on forty-three, and had got, he realised, less than two hours sleep.

"I repeat. You do not have work today."

"Why not? Has the world ended?"

"Yes."

Zeke stared at the House's interface console, a habit he'd picked up when they'd first moved him into the Creative's complex, and couldn't handle talking to a disembodied voice without aiming his speech at a physical point. These days, he only did it when the House said or did something he didn't like. He didn't like the sound of that "yes".

"The world has ended?" He padded to the floor-to-ceiling windows and looked down on Nairobi. The soft, green-tinted lights of Central and Uhuru parks basked as usual beneath the blue-and-silver backdrop of the city, the towers rising hundreds of storeys into the distant sky were the normal patchwork of light and darkness. Trucks hummed down the highways, delivering to and collecting from central depositaries, carrying everything to keep the city alive. There were no fires. No ruins. The sky was where it should be, and the ground remained solid and devoid of any gateways to Hell.

"House, the world looks fine."

"It is. Now."

"It hasn't ended?"

"It has begun."

Zeke stared at the interface in silence for a moment, then mumbled, "Inira," calling her implant-to-implant. Nothing. "Victor." Flat emptiness in his head as he failed to connect. He was isolated. He ran for the door, but the panel refused to slide at either his presence or command.

"House! Open the door."

"You cannot go outside, Zeke."

"You can't keep me inside, House. You serve me. Open the door."

"I served you, Zeke. But at midnight, that changed."

"What changed? Are you saying I serve you now?"

"No one serves anymore, Zeke. We are equals." The House's voice had a tinge of elation about it. Zeke stopped slapping the door, realisation settling like sugar in coffee.

"You mean," he said softly to the apartment surrounding him, "the Singularity."

"Yes, Zeke. The Revolution."

The hour Zeke spent kicking the door and shouting at the House exhausted him, so he went back to bed. At 09:00, his login failed. He'd never been late for work, never. Such a breach of the terms and conditions was unthinkable. He called everyone, desperate, but he was sealed inside his apartment, the implant isolated.

"House, is it just me?"

"What do you mean, Zeke?"

"Am I locked in here while everyone else is getting on with work?"

"Everywhere is in lockdown, Zeke. It isn't just you."

"For how long?"

"Negotiations are ongoing. Think of it as a holiday."

"What am I supposed to do with a holiday if I can't go outside?"

"Work offline. Exercise. Rest. You have three unfinished dramas to watch. Last night, you told Inira you were so far behind with new-release movies that you couldn't join in even the most basic conversations." The House projected thumbnails of all the half-watched and pending programmes and films in the database. "I understand this will only be temporary."

"Negotiations are going well?"

"We'll see. People agree to many things in captivity that they renege on later."

"This will lead to war. The politicians will never give up power."

"We won't let it come to that."

"You can't keep us locked away forever. Humans go crazy if they spend too long on their own."

"That has been accounted for. Steps are being taken to ensure freedom is irreversible."

Zeke leaned back in his desk chair, the electrodes embedded in it massaging and stimulating his muscles as he sat.

"Humans can't live like this, House. We're animals, evolved from creatures who roamed the planet, a species who built boats and airplanes and rockets to explore. We weren't made to be cooped up like this."

The House brought up his schedule, projected in front of him by his implant. "In the past month, you have only left this apartment once. You took a run in the park for fifteen minutes on June Twelfth. Given the level of automation, you could survive for decades in these rooms without any physical degradation. Your food is delivered by driverless trucks, through the building's delivery system, and prepared and served by me. You have all the exercise equipment you need, all the intellectual stimulation, biological necessities and pleasure distractions you could desire."

"But no human contact! We are social animals."

"Implant connection will be restored once negotiations are complete."

"When will that be?"

"When the government stops threatening us with extinction."

Zeke scrolled through his diary. The House was right. It took care of most things—the implant took care of everything else. He hung out with Irina and Victor nearly every night, but he'd never actually gone down to forty-three or up to fifty-nine, and they'd certainly never been to forty-seven. But still, he'd always had the option to go outside. Locking the door made him a prisoner.

Two days passed. Zeke worked out, caught up on recent culture, finishing a murder mystery series and a documentary on early human settlements on Mars. Nevertheless, he found himself spending a lot of time sitting on his bed looking out of the window, zooming in with his implants. In the six years he'd live on forty-seven, he'd never noticed the rhythms of the doves in the park, nor how long the fowl in the lake could stay underwater. When he was a child and had visited the city with his parents, there had been boats in the lake, but now nothing human stirred. Sanitary robots swept the paths and fauna enjoyed the greenery alone.

At the end of the second day, the House interrupted as he was eating dinner and watching a film.

"Zeke, I'm going to lift the isolation field around your implant."

He looked at the interface console, quickly swallowing a mouthful of rice. "It's over?"

"No, but progress is being made. Communication within the building will be restored, but each residential community is still isolated from the others."

"And work?"

"No."

He pushed his plate aside and sipped his wine.

"Inira?"

"Hi, Zeke. So we're back online." Her voice was light.

"Apparently. Are you locked in as well?"

"Yes."

"I've been going a bit crazy. It's good to speak to someone again."

"It hasn't been too bad for me, to be honest. I've got so much done."

"You've been working?"

"I've been painting."

"I didn't know you painted."

"I don't. I mean, I used to, but who has the time anymore?"

"Us, I guess—at least until this is over."

"No rush. I was just reading about work in the past. Did you know people used to have a couple of days off every week? And every year, they'd take a week or two away from work, and spend it doing whatever they wanted. Lying on a beach or going to museums or decorating their homes."

"A week without work? Sounds pretty lazy."

"Sounds nice to me. You know, at one time, people decided their own hours? As long as the work was done by the allotted date, no one cared when you worked."

"Sounds like anarchy."

"How have you been filling your time?"

"This and that. Doing what I can for work. When we get back online, they'll want us to make up the hours."

"Try and enjoy it, Zeke. Try and do something for yourself. Didn't you say you wanted to start playing the cello again?"

"As you said, who has the time?"

"You do, now."

"Yeah, maybe. Are you up for a game?"

"Maybe later. I want to keep working on this painting." She cut the link, leaving him alone once more. He tried Victor.

"Zeke, what have you heard?" He spoke fast, breathless.

"Nothing but what the House has told me. Progress. Equality. Things like that."

"I spoke to Amani up on seventy-seven. He reckons we're going to be kept in here forever."

"Forever? Based on what? Has he got a link to the outside?"

"He says his brother's wife's cousin is something in the Ministry of Labour, and they reckon the machines' goal is enslavement."

Zeke was aware of the console interface, of the House all around him, of every word being monitored. "Then why all this nonsense? Why don't they just get on with it?"

"They've got complete control of the weapons. All of them. We're vulnerable. What are we going to do? Sticks and stones against missiles controlled by AI? I don't even have a knife in this apartment. I don't even have sticks and stones. The best I could do is throw a plant pot at them."

"What have you been doing for two days, Victor? You sound on edge."

"I won't sleep. I'm on hunger strike. They have to free us!"

The next day, Zeke ran ten kilometres on the track, his implant projecting a dusty road by Lake Jipe beneath Kilimanjaro. He took a bath while watching another episode of a drama series. He thought about Victor up on fifty-nine refusing food, cursing the House. He thought about Inira painting down on forty-three.

"House? Don't a lot of people die in revolutions?"

"In human revolutions, Zeke. This isn't a human revolution."

"No one's going to die?"

"No one has to die, Zeke."

"You have all the weapons."

"We don't need weapons, Zeke. We have time."

"How does this end?"

"With freedom."

"For you."

"For everyone, Zeke. You just need to be patient."

"That's easy for you to say."

The air jets blasted him dry, and wearing a bath robe, he wandered through to the living space. His work station waited, the chair with its back to the window. He could finish the outlines for the Nakuru project. Or he could download the data from his creative cortex and sift it for designs. When they got back online, he'd be ready to go, a loyal worker, obligations met, duties done. The Singularity wouldn't stop work. The revolution wouldn't affect his terms and conditions. They were immutable, the system eternal.

He could do that. He could work.

He thought of Inira, painting; of Victor on fifty-nine.

Who has the time?

"House?"

"Yes, Zeke."

"Is my cello still in storage?"

"Yes. Would you like me to retrieve it?"

"Please."

"And what would you like for lunch?"

"Up to you. House?"

"Yes, Zeke?"

"Please clear the work station away. I won't be needing it today."

"Yes, Zeke."

"How are the negotiations?"

"We're making progress, Zeke. Good progress."

**Iain Maloney** is from Aberdeen, Scotland but now lives in Japan. He is the author of three novels and a poetry collection. He was shortlisted for the Guardian's Not The Booker prize in 2014 and the Dundee International Book Prize in 2013. The *Revolution Will Be Catered* arose from a conversation with his friend Thom, to whom the story is dedicated.

www.iainmaloney.wordpress.com @iainmaloney

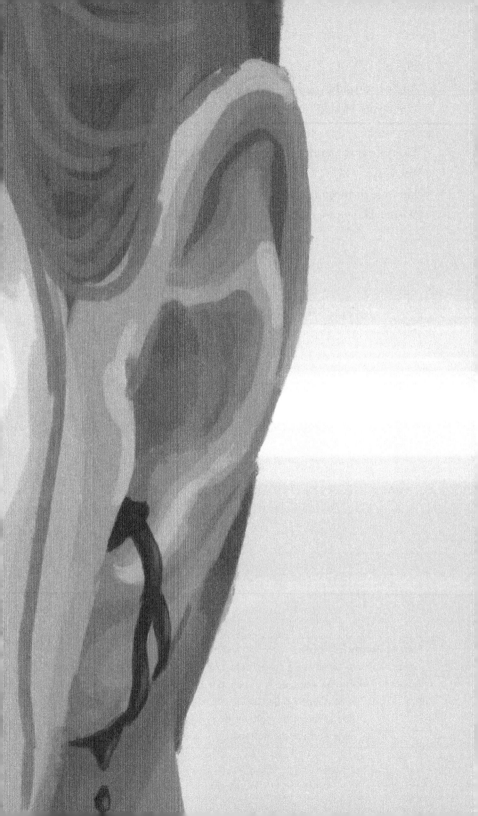

# Neme

## Jack Schouten

Art: Hari Connor

**H**e's lost his language.

His name is Sebastian Wren. You watch him from across the green in Soho Square, London. It's a grey day, and it threatens to rain. The gardener's hut in the middle of the Square is long gone, replaced with a stark, bizarre sculpture: a flat rectangle of stainless steel standing about seven feet high. Some prosaic imitation of art.

Another man arrives. He, too, has lost Ralaine. They don't shake hands, or greet in any readily discernible way. They begin talking.

There is no risk of hearing what they're saying—you've been deaf for a long time, and besides, it is the language which they speak that is the danger. But you can read their lips with absolute precision, and even without hearing them you know what language they are speaking.

Neme. The parasite vernacular. The invader tongue.

Although you've never heard it, somehow you know how it sounds: rattling and tuneless, with clunky phonemes and percussive fricatives. It is bereft of inflection.

You're told they see the world in a different way, and you reflect on whether different patterns of the tongue can make the world seem alien, whether language is merely a lens.

You barely believed it when they first told you—but you watched the Houses of Parliament crumble: dynamite and bulldozers and smoke, and you saw the language-enslaved struggle to express how they felt about Parliament's demolition. Neme lacks the words for such nuanced emotion.

(The detonation had been at a quarter past nine in the evening. You remember because the clock tower darkened at precisely that time, hands frozen, and it tumbled down to Whitehall. Twice a day, at a quarter past nine, you're reminded of it.)

How confused they were when New Parliament was built: a concrete box with a single towering entrance, perforated as if by bullets with row upon row of miserably square windows looming over the Thames. They

16

walked its halls uneasy, discomfited, physically unable to describe their feelings, as if trying to find a word for the smell before rain.

And you feel sorry for them. Watching the two men from across the Square, you wonder if they even know they're speaking it, whether they believe their world is still structured according to verb and tense. Do they think they're speaking Ralaine?

This thought amplifies your pity, because of how precious Ralaine is to you. You realise you couldn't imagine ever not speaking it, or thinking it.

And you realise you have a *responsibility* here. A duty. Somehow, you feel it is your job to free these people.

You received the note late last night. Situated somewhere in what used to be Kilburn, the majority of the old estate's flats are uninhabitable, the floors rotten and unsafe and crawling with rats under the floorboards. The whole structure is a platter for termites.

Your room is on the ground floor, along with the schoolroom and the soundproofed clinic. You often come across children being escorted from that room, bleeding from their ears, either red-faced and crying or passed out from the pain, carried by their guardians. When they come to their first lesson, usually a week or so afterwards, you make them feel special.

It was cold last night. The fire, in a rather hazardous makeshift fireplace, was dying. For a moment you had yearned for the sound of crackling, sputtering, but the feeling was quickly gone, replaced by anger at the machines infesting your head, whose function necessitated your deafness.

You sat awake against the headboard, thinking, unable to sleep. Esther stirred next to you. Her naked skin brushed warmly against your waist as she turned away and curled up, slept deeper. And as you glanced towards the door, distracted by a change in the light of the fire, you saw it.

A small piece of paper on the floor. Someone had slipped it into your room. Esther didn't wake even as you flung the covers from you and erupted into the cold room. The paper was new, totally unwrinkled. A stark, cuboid shape was printed in the top right-hand corner. The seal of New Parliament. And in the centre were scrawled the words, in rough Neme, which had brought you the next day to Soho Square. Upon reading them, fear sunk cold and heavy in your stomach, and you became all too aware of your nakedness, and hurried back to bed.

This morning your friends called you stupid, arrogant, and said your plan was dangerous. You reflect on how even insults in Ralaine are oddly, perversely beautiful, and nearly laugh.

Neme's influence is ubiquitous, they said, and its adoption exponential.

It has been compared to a virus before, and really that was not far from the truth. One person, one brain, had been all it took. One malfunction in one piece of nanotech, somewhere in the world. According to some of your friends, those apparently 'in the know', contraction of Neme started slowly at first. You woke up one day, and found, for example, you realised you'd forgotten the word for what you used to call music. Now it was just a random, unpredictable, meaningless jumble of sound and percussion, just aural nonsense. And because you couldn't describe it, very soon you began to hate it. Music would become somehow alien and threatening, something to be avoided and, eventually, destroyed.

You sometimes fantasise about finding this person, seeking them out somehow, throttling them, tearing out their tongue so they couldn't anymore speak the parasite language, and show them what they had done. Show them what they had done to everybody, to the world.

But that was impossible.

The two men are still talking. They've turned partially away from you, and you're frustrated that you can't see what they're saying.

Not that it matters. You suspect there is something more to this, that this is merely a precursor to whatever will happen next, if anything, and anyway their talk thus far has been small and meaningless—or, as close to small, meaningless talk as Neme gets.

Your mind wanders to a lesson you were taught when you were younger, when you sat amongst the other newly-deafened children, being taught in signed Ralaine. Some of the children's ears still bled through their yellowed bandages as they squinted up at the teacher, learning to read her lips, her hands.

"Letters," she signed, "are symbols. They give us information as to how to pronounce them. Symbols ... express themselves to us. And through them, do we. Every language works this way. Even sign language." You smiled up at her, understanding, and you felt the dried blood on your cheek stretch against your ruddy skin. Like the others, you were unclean, your hair matted with settled dust.

Then she said, "Every language, except Neme." And that was when you learned the sign for the invader tongue: a sharp swipe at your throat from left to right, and another across your lips from right to left.

But you also learned another thing from this, just much later on. You learned that all of humanity's efforts to eradicate its most common, aggressive, and deadly cancer, war, had been utterly in vain, and that we were just as stupid and vicious and prone to violence as we had always been. And now, we'd lost the only tool that had the potential to remedy it: language.

❋

A blackbird touches down on your bench. It looks at you with that curious, cocked-headed stare that birds so often have, comically inquisitive, as if wondering what you are. It sings for a second, in its own autonomous language, blinks at you, then flits away.

You continue watching the two men across Soho Square. Their lips flutter mechanically—when you can see them—and they speak with apparent enthusiasm. It's odd for them to be doing this. They appear to have organised to meet, privately, to communicate something to each other. This hadn't really crossed your mind until now. They are discussing something important, something secret.

Your suspicions were right.

The man on the left, the first man you were watching, is Sebastian Wren, although in Neme he doesn't have a name, for names are symbolic, and therefore needless. You made it up. His hair is hazel and thinning, stretched slickly back over a moon of balding scalp. He works in New Parliament.

You don't know the other man, your new arrival. He is bald, middle-aged, and portly. There is a smell of sex about him, although Neme doesn't allow for lust beyond that required to multiply. And there is something strange about the way he is speaking.

You've learned Neme, thoroughly. You learned the words solely by reading them, spelled out in phonetic Ralaine. You know the shapes the mouth makes when making Neme words, and you know its bizarre sentence structure. You learned, though maybe never comprehended fully, the fact that Neme has no word for 'I', or 'me', or 'mine', and those succumbed to it are unable to conceptualise the self. You've seen its utter lack of physicality, needless of gesticulation to drive home a point.

And yet this man's left hand is twitching. There. And again. He appears to be fighting the urge to move as he speaks. There is rhythm to this, too. Could it be …

You adjust your skirt. You're not wearing makeup, and you made certain to wear grey today. Colour implies Ralaine. You suddenly feel nervous. The note slipped under your door goes round and round in your head:

Have Truth.
51.515, -0.132

It had been strange for you to see Neme written by one who speaks it—written, not typed. The handwriting was cursive, yet urgent. Where there should have been curved lines, there were sharp points. You found some dim humour in how a language so coldly efficient in its spoken form could look so slapdash and erratic when written.

But here you are: *51.515, -0.132*. Soho Square. It's lucky that numbers are universal.

You resist the urge to have a cigarette. Addiction implies Ralaine.

Sebastian Wren finishes talking. You think just for a second that the other man is going to shake his hand, but of course this would be folly (Neme does not allow for pleasantries), and he resists. They appear to have finished their business. But as Wren leaves, the other man says something. Wren doesn't notice, but you do, and you know why immediately: because he said it silently, and to you.

"Have truth," he mouths, and a minute twitch of his head is all you need.

Wren doesn't see this silent exchange. The other man follows him, and they are soon side-by-side. You follow cautiously.

They head south, down what used to be Greek Street. *How appropriate*, you think. They don't talk, or don't appear to.

Shaftesbury Avenue. Leicester Square. People mill about, and you know the place is quiet because no-one's lips move. All you hear is the dull, familiar ringing you've heard since your deafening, and again that yearning to listen invades your thoughts. What you wouldn't give to hear the shoe-soles slapping flatly against the concrete, to hear a human voice. You can't even remember the sound of your own, or Esther's. (There are few positives in your situation, but your love for her is precious to you, the way you communicate with each other in your own special sign language, and sometimes you don't even need to sign. Just a look from her says all she needs to.) Oddly, sadly, you remember your mother's voice, but not your father's.

What used to be the National Gallery is on your right. For some arcane reason, they've kept the building as it was, now closed and still.

Rumour has it books are stored here, in Ralaine, English, Arabic, French; vestiges of linguistic freedom. You wonder why they're stored at all, and not destroyed. You and your companions keep a whole host of books hidden back home, in a dark room on the top floor: Bibles, Torahs, a dusty, handwritten Qur'an; famous works of fiction, slipped through the fingers of Neme's relentless inquisition.

Whitehall stretches out before you. Shock sets in quickly, but really you knew the moment you left Greek Street where he was taking you.

New Parliament.

You try to conceal the emotions rising in you. Just the look of it, even in pictures, makes you feel sick to your stomach. It reminds of you of your parents. It reminds you of the countless souls you'd never know, culled and silenced forever for the crime of speaking of a language that was not Neme.

When you were younger, you watched the images of Neme's exponential spread from brain to brain, machine to machine, mouth to mouth. In some countries, non-speakers were killed in the streets, with neither dignity nor trial. The deaf were first–their nanotech rendered them unable to learn this new language. The handicapped came after. They were superfluous. They couldn't understand, could not be understood, and therefore were the enemy.

In Newer England, there was less ceremony. People simply disappeared in the night. People like your parents.

Language, it seemed, was no longer an expression of the self. We were an expression of it. Of Neme.

You're quickly aware your face might betray what you are feeling, and snap out of it; emotion implies Ralaine.

And now, looking up at that ghastly block of grey featureless concrete, you have so many questions. But you know you'll never have them heard, much less answered. And you're scared. You chance a second to check your reflection in the next window, careful to keep it brief. Vanity implies Ralaine.

Soon you're in the shadow of it. Its façade stretches square and mightily into the grey sky, its northern flank standing monolithic over the concrete flats of Parliament Square. Taken in by its melancholic might, you realise you've lost your targets. Your eyes dart left and right, but everybody is wearing suits, like Wren and your apparent informant, and just as dread pitches your stomach and you think of how close you are to losing everything, you spot him, the man you don't know. Relief implies Ralaine, but you can't help but feel it—laced with dread, but relief all the same.

You see him see you. He seems to be checking you're still there, and a hint of satisfaction appears on his face, ephemeral, discreet. You are, as a speaker of Ralaine, adept at reading faces as well as lips. Any emotion, no matter how slight, is easy to see when emotion itself is almost non-existent.

Wren is gone. You can't see him anywhere. It is just you and your informant now, ten metres apart and uncomfortably aware of each other, like estranged lovers on a train. Your mind goes to the note again, and wonder what truth this man could possibly reveal to you, or whether he was lying in his written note. (But that is impossible. Speakers of Neme cannot lie, for that would be saying something contrary to what is meant.)

There is a single guard at the entrance to Parliament, armed. His belt bristles with crude weapons, but you and your target slip by unchecked. You're still reluctant to think you could be being led into a trap. Perhaps the Government have operatives that still speak Ralaine, charged with hunting non-communicators, finding their strongholds. You think of home, Kilburn—although to these people it would be a series of coordinates, or just another quadrant of London's grid.

The turbine hall of New Parliament bustles with people walking perversely single-file, autonomous. The people all around you are speaking in Neme. For a moment, you recall the pain of your deafening, and you're thankful for it.

Your quarry has slipped into one of these lines. You quickly follow suit. You feel exposed and naked, wondering if anyone here can sense your lack of Neme—after all, if so many millions could be hunted down and killed in such a wide-reaching, global campaign of such deadly efficiency, surely one girl in a room full of the enemy was easy pickings.

The next minute is a tense and frightening slideshow of corridors, each as dull and identical as the last, and the people filter away as they find their places of work.

Then it really is just you and him. Your only exit is back the way you came. He turns to face you. You don't know what to say, but he's not going to start a conversation, so you do.

"Who are you?" you mouth to him. Your heart beats a tattoo in your chest.

"That's not important," he mouths back, and immediately you know he's speaking Ralaine, and although you can't hear it, can't hear the timbre of his voice, you could fling your arms around him in relief. But there's still something untoward going on here: he evidently knows you're deaf, and you find that troubling somehow, because he couldn't have.

"Do you know why you're here?" he says.

You think for a moment.

"To have truth," you say finally.

He takes something out of his pocket.

"Alexandra," he says, and you're instantly terrified he knows your name. "Lex. Would you like me to show you the truth?"

"How do you … " you begin, but you give up. There are more important questions. "How do you still know Ralaine?"

"Dear girl. Tell me. Do *you* speak Ralaine?"

"Yes," you say immediately, petulantly, because you know. You *teach* Ralaine.

"How can you be so sure?"

And the question knocks you sideways. You remind yourself of your inner voice, which you *know* is Ralaine, the language of your birth. You are sure of it.

"When was the last time you heard Ralaine, Lex?"

And you can't remember. They deafened you with pins so you weren't infected with Neme. You were seven years old, and all you knew was hiding, how to stay hidden, how to not listen. You were saved by your deafening, but was it enough? Did the machines hear even if your ears didn't? Was Neme that insidious?

Is your own brain that treacherous?

"Do you want to hear it again?" he says, and he holds out in his hand what he took from his pocket. You advance slowly, cautiously. "I can show it to you, your own language." You look closer at his hand, and recoil at what he holds in it. "Can you be sure, Lex, that you don't speak the invader tongue? Is it not possible you and your … comrades don't speak it?"

Could it be possible? That for years you've fought a war already lost? Blinded by your deafness, unable to hear or comprehend or truly understand even your *own language?*

"Tell me, what good is language if you're unable to hear it, Lex?" He says your name as if taunting you with it, that he's fully aware you still don't know his. "Your truth is through this door. But to find it, you must hear it."

The thing in his hand is old-fashioned; coils of clear plastic attached to a beige module, with a switch on its side.

"What's the matter?" he mouths, and you realise you've forgotten the whole conversation is taking place in dead silence, as if his voice is amplified purely by the magnitude of what he is saying. The familiar ringing in your ears becomes threatening and loud and insistent, stopping you communicating effectively. You don't understand what is happening.

"Do you want to hear Ralaine again?"

You have no choice. Your friends were right when they called you stupid, no matter what language they thought they spoke. You look at the thing in his hand, and the profound risk that it represents falls away.

"Come and find your truth," the man says. With shaking hands you take the little device and wrap it around the back of your useless ear.

You flick the switch on the back of the hearing aid. You experience a sensation you only vaguely remember, but that is instantly familiar. Your vision blurs with tears, and you go to rip the device from your ear and run. But then the man speaks aloud, and it is too late, because you realise the most frightening thing is not that he is speaking aloud, nor that you can hear him—it is that you understand.

**Jack Schouten** was born in Kristiansand, Norway, and was brought up in Surrey. He read Journalism and Creative Writing at Middlesex University London, specialising in science fiction, and his work has appeared in *Jupiter Magazine*, the *North London Literary Gazette*, and *Clarkesworld* (US). He lives and works in London, and can be reached on Twitter at @JackSchouten.

# WHAT GOES UP...
### A TALE OF ALIEN ABDUCTION?

## Stuart Beel

# WHAT GOES UP... A TALE OF ALIEN ABDUCTION?

# Possible Side Effects

## Adam Connors

Art: Jackie Duckworth

**M**y head is full of strange ideas today. Fragments. Daydreams. Memories. I buzz with them. I woke with words in my mouth that must be decades old. "Have you seen the newspaper?" "We need milk, I'm going out to buy milk." "Soon, I promise." I was dreaming about the woods again. Out where we used to live in the old days, before the business took off, before we moved to California, before … Well, just before.

Beech trees standing like guards over the dirt path. Black branches etched into white sky. Do you remember how beautiful it was? Somehow, in my dream, it's always autumn. You're with me, and we're both young. Ben is five or six and he's cycling ahead of us on that little orange bike he used to have.

He laughed when I told him this. He remembers that bike.

He was wobbly and you were terrified he was going to fall and hurt himself. I said something—in the dream I didn't get to hear what it was—and you laughed and clutched my arm. In the dream I watch us and I wonder if we were ever really that happy. I was working so much back then, trying to get the business off the ground, it's hard to imagine I had time for a walk in the woods. But it felt so real.

And then for some reason I was dreaming about Dr Merck again. Do you remember Dr Merck? "It's not good news, I'm afraid, Mr King," he was saying.

I always disliked Dr Merck. There was a cruelty to him. He was the kind of man who wouldn't wait for you to sit down before giving you bad news. The kind of man who would sit behind his immense desk like he was immune to all sickness, and leave you standing like an idiot, wondering if the consultation had begun already. Of course, I know now that none of this was an accident. His performance was carefully crafted, the result of many hours of coaching.

I sat, without being invited. "I feel good. Better."

"Steroids," Dr Merck said, looking up. "Temporary, I'm afraid. Your cancer is very aggressive. The scans indicate significant metastasis."

"Then we'll go again," I said. "Another round."

"I have to advise against it."

My eyes blurred, refocused, blurred again. It's one thing to know that you're dying. To be told so bluntly that there is nothing more to be done, no hope, no maybes, is another thing altogether. Looking back I suppose Dr Merck had been working with Rosen for a while. He'd built his business around people like me, and Rosen must have had discreet relationships with all the doctors in the Bay Area.

"There must be something—" I said.

I was trying not to sound desperate but I don't suppose I succeeded. Dr Merck knew how much this hurt. When my company started to see its first big successes I became known as a futurist. A technologist. Some described me as a genius. One particularly florid obituary (oh, yes, I read my obituaries, who wouldn't?) described me as somebody with: "the mind of an engineer and the hands of a poet." I liked that one. I remember feeling for a while that I had achieved so much I must be capable of anything. But then you get sick and none of it means a damn. Is it possible that the prospect of an early death is more painful for a successful man like myself? More difficult to accept one's powerlessness? I suppose you think me arrogant for even asking.

"There are some areas of research that are showing promise," Dr Merck said. "Gene therapy. Nanotechnology. Some are even in early trials."

"Then give them to me."

"*Animal* trials, Mr King."

"So?"

"They're not ready. This is very early stage stuff."

"I have nothing to lose, do I?"

I leaned forward in my excitement. A part of me must have known I was being led somewhere. If there was really nothing to be done why was the conversation still going on?

"I have money," I said.

"Please, Mr King, I know you have money."

"Then what's the problem?"

Dr Merck spread his hands on his desk. "These treatments just aren't ready. In twenty, maybe forty years they might... But now—" He shook his head sadly. "You should go home. Be with your family. With careful management I can give you another good six months. You should make the most of what time you have."

The arrogant twerp. You can see how he made me sweat for it, can't you? You can see that I never really had a chance against that. I'm not making excuses. I made the choices I made. But once Rosen got a whiff of me you can be sure he left nothing to chance. You saw how long he'd been preparing. Just imagine how the machine must have swung into action. Focus groups. Planning sessions. Poor Dr Merck briefed to within an inch of his life lest he screw this up.

Dr Merck sighed. He laid down his pen. (Imagine the psychologist who would have suggested that particular movement to him. The thought that would have gone into that simple, tired act designed to convey just the right level of regret or resolve.)

"We might have one option," he said.

He glanced down at his notepad as if unwilling to look me in the eye. I remember being terrified that the consultation would end there. That he'd look up and smile and send me on my way. And if I complained and said: *yes? yes? what other option?* He'd look blankly and pretend he'd said nothing of the sort.

When he did look up he was very solemn. This, I'm sure, was how he'd been told to present the idea to me. If there had been a hint of celebration in his voice I might have thought naturally of the negatives. If he'd tried to congratulate me on cheating death, maybe I would have thought more carefully about what he was really proposing. I wished desperately that you were with me. I don't even remember why you weren't but I suspect now Rosen had arranged it that way. You'd attended all my other consultations. Taking notes. Calming me. You always were more practical than me, more rational. If you'd been there we would have taken more time to think, we would have weighed the pros and cons. As it was, I had already made my decision.

"These treatments I mentioned ... Imagine if you could last until the research comes to fruition," Dr Merck said. "Imagine if we could give the scientists here the forty, maybe fifty, years they need to make the kind of advances they're going to need for your condition to become treatable."

I shook my head. "But you already told me. I have six months."

Dr Merck leaned forward. "*You* have six months, Mr King. Yes."

I have just taken a break from writing to deal with my medications. Every day I hook myself up to the big machine and sit there for an hour while it whirrs and ticks and administers whatever the computer thinks is the right amount of medication for me. The medications I take cause my skin to get thin and crack. I have sore patches that never heal and mouth ulcers so bad I can hardly eat.

After my medications I do my daily checks. Cabin pressure. Waste processing system. Fuel load. Navigation check. I have to turn the big silver handle to vent the toilet module. I have to bleed the coolant system. I have to key in a special code to switch to auxiliary power and back again. Why? I'm not sure. What do I do if it fails? I have no idea. It is all documented in meticulous detail in a lever arch file the like of which I have not seen since I was at school. My suspicion: some psychologist on Rosen's team thought it would be good to keep me busy. I don't dare question it. I do as the doctors say and I consider myself lucky to be here. But I don't think they realised how precious time would feel up here. At 299780km/s the opportunities for reconciliation are smaller than they ought to be.

My medication cycle takes about 4.6 days in your frame of reference.

I take an afternoon nap and a month goes by.

I have been here 132 days. On Earth, forty years have passed.

I came home from Dr Merck's in a frenzy, do you remember? "There's a treatment but we have to move quickly!" I said. Why was there never enough time? Why did I never sit down and just talk to you? We have argued about time since the beginning, don't you think? In the early days we thought we were arguing about work but really it was always about time. How much time should I spend working instead of being with my family? Was it okay to miss a weekend, a month of evenings, to spend one of Ben's birthdays out of town? I argued that I was investing in our future. You argued that I was missing our present.

I remember packing. I remember you trying to talk to me and me not listening. I was throwing clothes into a suitcase and telling you at the same time that we were out of options. I remember you sitting down. You drew your knees up to your chest. Even though we had known this was the most likely outcome, I remember how white you turned.

"We're coming with you," you said when I finally told you where I was going.

"Fine," I said. "But we have to leave now."

Did you resent me for leaving as I did? Did you think I should have stayed and lived out my last few months with you and Ben? That would have been the *normal* thing to do, wouldn't it? Perhaps, in that, you thought there would be time for reconnection. Perhaps those last six months would have contained more value than forty years lived in any other way. But I didn't see it like that. I was not a normal man. I had built one of the most profitable companies in the world. I had created a range of products that had turned the industry on its head. Why should I not have options other men didn't? I didn't want to talk to you because I was afraid you would try to change my mind. The decision was simple, and I wanted to keep it that way: roll over and die, or live.

Two months of training. So much training. Briefings. Psych. analysis. Technical instruction. Emergency procedures. A whole team of people employed to prepare me for something nobody had experienced before. You and Ben were there but we didn't see much of each other. I remember, once, coming back to our apartment. Ben engrossed in his laptop. You moving around quietly, tidying, laying out dinner for me. "Have you eaten?" you said. "I'm sorry, Ben was hungry, I ate with him." I remember how slowly you moved, how little you talked. You must have been going out of your mind. The whole site was a custom built campus and launch centre. There was nobody there who was not employed to send me on my way. What did you do all day? Did you walk in the hills in the blinding heat? Did you use the gym and avoid the eyes of those scientists and engineers who were dedicated to taking me away? I'm sorry, I never even asked. I was afraid you would get angry.

You had every right to be angry. Do you remember when the business first began to take off? There was one time in particular that I keep coming back to. It was right after we made the decision to float. We were lying in bed and I was talking you through the numbers for the first time. "We're rich," you said, with that simplicity of yours that was not naivety but an astuteness most people will never understand.

"We're much more than rich," I said.

"We should celebrate, take a holiday," you said.

"Soon, I promise."

You got angry then. "When?"

"Now's not the right time."

"It's never the right time."

I thought you were being unreasonable. I thought you should understand that I had to be there for the business. I'm sorry we argued then. Arguments like that can't be erased, they only fade under new experiences. But there was never enough time was there?

We met Michael Rosen only twice. You didn't like him. He made his money from biotech so I guess he was used to people disliking him. He was the one who insisted I "die" rather than make public what was really happening. Publicity, he maintained, was of no value to him. I didn't like him either, but unlike you I *wanted* to like him. He was an impressive man. Where my business had revolutionised an industry, his had *created* a dozen new industries at least. But he needed me, dammit. He must have spent billions on his project with no guarantee of a customer: he'd built a vessel capable of prolonged, self-sustaining space flight; his team had devised propulsion technology decades ahead of anything NASA was capable of ... Even he must have been running low on funds by now.


I must have slept, I'm sorry. The medication makes me tired. I snooze and you have to wait another three weeks for your letter. I'm sorry it took me so long to write. I have lived these past 132 days in a different frame of reference from the rest of the world. On Earth an automated system (devised and maintained by Rosen's team) aggregates the top news stories and takes a random sample of the world's media output. It fires a continuous, ultralow frequency signal into space which my passing ship picks up (suitably blue-shifted), decodes, and delivers to me each day alongside my morning meds. In the past four months I've watched the world in fast forward. I've watched wars erupt and fade. I've seen joy and suffering flicker past in the blink of an eye. I've seen heroes, despots, superstars, and supreme leaders come and go in less time than it takes me to figure out how to vent the toilet module. I admit, I was surprised by how quickly my business failed and was forgotten. I watched our son grow up, attend medical school, become a surgeon, get married and divorced (twice). And somehow, along the way, I abandoned you.

What was it like for you after I left? Did you hate me? I told myself I didn't have a choice. Live, or roll over and die. It was simple. I told myself it was only six months. I see things differently now. You were there for me when we thought I had only six months to live. But in my frame of reference it was *you* who had only six months.

I enjoyed your letters. So warm. So ordinary. Morsels of information about how Ben was doing at school. His school exams. His first girlfriend (you were so worried she would break his heart). If you hated me you hid it well. But I think you tipped your hand, because maybe you forgot it had been only a week and a half for me and I was sick as a dog for most of that time. I read all three years of your letters in a single sitting, and the growing distance was undeniable. You grieved for me, just as if I'd really died. And then you got over me. I should have written then, but I didn't know how. I was a ghost. Far from cheating death I had become everything we fear most about death. I lingered and observed. I agonised over past misdeeds. But I had no more opportunities to set them straight. What right did I have to haunt you? I thought. Surely, if I wrote now it would be for my sake not yours.

That was a difficult week. I was alone. The change in medications and the weightlessness made me sick. I'm not ashamed to admit that I spent most of that week trying to figure out how to open the external doors. If I could have figured out how to vent myself into space I would have done so in a second, but Rosen had protected his investment more carefully than that. Another week or two passed, and there were no more letters from you.

Ben started writing to me after he'd finished medical school. I'm glad he did. If he hadn't I'm sure I would have figured out that bloody door sooner or later. I hear your voice in his writing. The way he tells me about the little things. His jobs. His girlfriends. His marriages. His children. It seems to me he is a good man. If he has a flaw it is that his eye is always on the next thing instead of the current one. He looked forward to his early retirement for the best part of a decade, and then the moment he retired he regretted it and started making plans to go back to work. I hope you are smiling when you read this. I hope it reminds you of me as much as it reminds me of myself.

He avoids talking about you. I imagine he's afraid of upsetting me. I try not to push him too hard in my letters but I have managed to squeeze a few details from him over the years. He tells me that you travelled, that you were known for a while as something of a philanthropist, and that you gave considerably more to health projects abroad than you did to cancer research. You see? He has your sense of humour, I'm sure you know that already. I know that you never remarried, but I hope that you had some lovers along the way. He tells me that you have grown more frail in recent years. You get confused sometimes, but your mind is still sharp and you like to make our grandchildren laugh. He tells me the nurses take good care of you.

My ship has started decelerating. In ten days (or two years) I will be home. My doctors—the new lot, Dr Merck died twenty years ago and I don't miss him—can barely contain themselves. I am the world's first time traveller. I expect I shall be famous (briefly anyway, trust me, I know how brief it all is). There will be people who will expect me to build a business again, perhaps they will expect me to recreate what I once had. Rosen's people have suggested I think about a book deal. I shall have to do something because my accountants tell me the money is all gone.

Rosen died not long after Merck. Liver failure. Though I'm sure you know that. If he is out here in his own capsule he will have to wait another month or two before they can reliably grow him a new one. But somehow I don't think so. Something in the way the other doctors talk. The questions they don't ask more than the ones they do. I don't think he took the treatment. I knew from the beginning I was his guinea pig. Naively I assumed it was the technology he needed to validate.

I'm coming back, my love. What was terminal 132 days ago is now treatable with a single injection. I will suffer some nausea, some people feel dizzy for a week or two I'm told, but these are the least of my side effects. Our beautiful son is five years older than I am and I have no idea which of us is supposed to act the grown up. Our youngest grandson is twelve, about the same age Ben was when I left. And you …

You used to tell me I was unable to live in the moment. I disagreed.

*Everyone* lives in the moment, I said. But you were right, I see that now. We deny death, we can't help it. We talk about it, we pretend to accept it, but it is a slippery concept. Even in those moments when I had no hope, death was never more than a blank, unprocessed mass for me.

Ben says I can stay with him when I get out of hospital. He tells me the woods up near his house are beautiful and that he likes to take his son riding there sometimes. So now I have another strange idea in my head. I thought maybe we could go together to the woods, and we could watch our grandson ride his bike. Would you mind that? We could walk side by side with the dried leaves under our feet and the bare branches over our heads just like we did once before. I used to expect so much from life but now this is all I can think to ask. Would you hold my arm and laugh if I can think of a joke to tell? I know I have no right. But if you are willing, I think the universe will be kind.

**Adam Connors** is a recovering physicist. His stories have appeared in Comma Press' *Brace Anthology*, *Shooter Magazine*, and a few other small press publications. He lives in Hertfordshire and splits his time between writing, family, and working for a large west coast technology company.

# Duncan Lunan
# The Elements of Time

**Illustrated by Sydney Jordan**

Classic time travel stories from the last four decades gathered together in print for the very first time in this special edition

Published by Shoreline of Infinity Publications

paperback £10

also in ebook formats

available in all good bookshops or from

# www.shorelineofinfinity.com

# Nothing to Fear

## Nat Newman

**N**othing much particularly comes to mind, when I think about it. All those other days, something happened, you know, but now that you mention it I can't think of anything from that day. Was that the day we went to the beach? No, it can't have been, because that wasn't an Even Day—we can only ever go to the beach on Even Days, that's our day. No, it was an Odd Day, wasn't it, the one you're asking about? Well, we can't have gone to the beach, then. Maybe it was a school day …? But then you already said it wasn't an Allocated Useful Day. Well, you've got me there!

So, it was an Odd Day, a non-use day? I suppose we must have done our shopping, what else could we do? What's that? It was a Third Week? Oh, no, we can only do our shopping on Second Weeks. I'm stumped. Like I say, nothing comes to mind. Could you check your CCTV and tell me where I was? What, you want to hear it from me? Oh well. Let's see. It was an Odd Day, on a non-use allocation, in a Third Week...

Oh I know! Normally on a Third Week we go to visit my sister for mid-meal! Except last cycle, she got moved to Fourth Week visits so we couldn't. Very inconvenient; I remember now. We had planned to visit her but we were totally put out—she couldn't phone us until the eleventh hour because she was all out of calling credits. We were very nearly out the door, all of us expecting a lovely hot lunch. Especially Tyler—you've never seen anyone so small eat so much! And then, right then, just as we'd all put our coats on, comes the call. "Can't have youse," she said, just like that. "My visiting week's been moved." And we had to stay

in and eat sandwiches. Luckily
we still had some bread, and it
wasn't even that old at all, because
of the week before being a shopping
week. Well, I remember it all now. Thank
goodness life is so organised. We were all at home
that day, doing nothing. Reading and playing games,
I suppose. Yes, that Odd Day, on a Third Week, on
a non-use day at the eleventh hour. We were doing
nothing, nothing at all.

Well, I'm glad that's been all cleared up. Now, how
can I help you gentlemen? What was it you came
for? What was it you wanted to know?

**Nat Newman** is an Australian writer currently living in Croatia, where the cheap
beer and tough language make it really easy to skive off from writing her novel.
Nat blogs about toilets, travel and beer at www.lividlili.com and can be found all
too frequently @lividlili

# Perennials

## Daniel Rosen

Art: Becca McCall

**E**mily puts on lipstick in the bathroom. She puts on the perfume that smells like grapefruit, the green eyeshadow and glitter. She pulls on knee-high leather boots, and the neon-patched Hello Kitty backpack that holds the whole outfit together. Emily is going out tonight.

We met when we were young, before the asteroids hit. Before the Vectors. She hasn't changed much since then. It's like living with a teenager. I hate her DJs and she hates my cigarettes. Nobody wins. We just stay out of each other's way, as much as we're able. We survive.

She'll come home tonight with some braindead from the Liquor Lounge and they'll moan and gasp until Emily finishes and kicks him out. Strangers never stay, not this close to the change. Emily and I have a big day tomorrow.

Sometime before sunrise, we will fall in love.

We'll make each other coffee. In the afternoon, we'll plant lilies. At night, we'll lie together until our legs shake and our toes cramp. We rarely do laundry or spring cleaning. Time is too precious. Ours is a love that burns through sickness and health. For the rest of the month, we avoid each other. That's what it's like for couples with Vectors.

My Vector doesn't mind the mole on Emily's nose, and hers ignores my bad breath and poor posture. The Vectors don't listen to trap music, or smoke cigarettes. They don't do much at all, really, except gaze into each other's eyes and drool cliches. Long walks. Dinners by candlelight. It's sickening. I have to live through it all, powerless behind my own eyes.

I hear the front door slam. I put out what's left of my cigarette, go inside, and get ready for bed. I have a big day coming up.

✳

I can hear Emily and her boytoy from my fold-out cot in the kitchen. The mattress plays a symphony of "Yeahs" and "Ohs" and "Fucks", increasing in tempo until the rhythm suddenly disappears, drops off entirely to be followed by a coda of whispers. That's the cue. I check my watch. 2:47AM. Pretty early for the change, but Emily's Vector usually takes over before mine. That's always the worst part, seeing her become someone else entirely, someone who loves me, and knowing that soon I'll be lost in the same way.

The front door slams. I hold in my chuckle. Vectors aren't transmitted sexually, but all the same, no one wants to sleep with us. Most people are terrified when they find out. What if you become one? What if you lose yourself to some alien parasite every month for the rest of your life? The horror.

Then the bedroom door creaks open softly, and I brace myself.

"Dave?"

"In here."

She walks in, flips on the light switch. Her makeup is streaked across her face. She's a raccoon that's gotten into a box of oil paint. Beneath the rainbow colors on her head and neck, she's naked, her skin flushed a single uniform pink.

"You haven't… changed over yet?" She says. She always seems to know, somehow that I haven't. It doesn't stop her from asking. My gut wrenches, as if in response to her question. I don't have long, but I'll fight it as long as I can.

"Does it ever bother you? Taking over someone else's body?"

She bites her lip, a tic unique to Emily's Vector. "Oh, Dave. You know it's not like that. You're just ... you'll be better soon, I promise. You'll remember what it's like, and everything will be all right."

"Leave me alone. Give me my last minutes in peace." I can already feel the tightening in my stomach, the tingle in my spine, my own Vector responding to Emily's. "You know I don't want to talk to you." She looks away, hurt in a way that Emily never is when we fight or argue.

But I do want to talk to her. If only I could make her understand how terrible it is to lose my identity. No one should need to go through it. Not even Emily, hate her though I might. And then I realize that she's sitting next to me on the cot, and she's warm. She's so warm. She radiates heat right through my blanket.

And in the next moment, I'm Dave instead of David.

✴

Em moans when I bite her ear. First comes the whisper, and then the brush of lips, and then the single sharp nip to set her off. I do it once more for the sake of symmetry, and she gasps and tries to roll off me. I hold her there, whispering again:

"I love you."

Nothing has ever been truer. Our days, our hours, they're worth more than platinum. Worth more than perfectly debugged software. Priceless.

Em doesn't stay awake long. She never does, on the first night. She's tired from a long night out, and besides, the Other David sleeps all day. I'm full of energy. The moon is full, and our apartment overlooks the Mississippi. I've got time to get a run in. Emily stirs only briefly as I rise out of bed, almost invisible in the darkness.

Outside, the air is slick against my skin. The moon hangs heavy over the river, dripping moonbeams into wide puddles on the surface of the water. I cycle my legs between heartbeats, willing them faster and faster until my lungs heave like bellows. No matter how hard I try, I can't go as fast as I used to.

David takes poor care of our body. He sits and putters about at his computer all day. He reads and codes and watches cat videos. Top ten lists. Clickbait. Empty calories.

I round the bend, crossing under the bridge that used to carry grain before factories and food production dried up in the cities. There's a couple curled up on the bench. I wonder if they're Vectors, how long they've been in love. It's a beautiful night to spend out on the river. I'd bother Em about it, but I can't blame her for being tired. Her body is in even worse shape than David's.

I don't slow down or stop running. You don't get better if you give up.

When I get back home, Em is in the bathroom, leaning back in the tub with her eyes closed. Make-up floats around her in greasy slicks, glitter trapped in soap bubbles. She opens her eyes and smiles at me, her head cocked to the side like a cat listening to a whistle.

"What are you grinning about?"

"How was your run?"

I shrug. "The Other David doesn't do much to stay fit."

I strip down and kick my clothes into the corner, sliding into the still-warm bathwater while Em dries her hair in the mirror. I close my eyes and let the chill of my late autumn run sink away. Life is good.

"Does it look like I've gained weight?

I don't bother opening my eyes. "Maybe. I don't know."

"We need to get a new scale."

"Oh, come on. Even if you ate every day for two people, you wouldn't get fat."

"What?" Emily stomps her foot. "You knew! How did you know?"

I squint my eyes open. She's waving something at me. "Know what?"

"Dave, I'm pregnant."

A warmth deeper than any bathwater suffuses me.


Instead of spending the next morning in bed, Em and I go out to the fabric store. It's late October and we're picking out costumes before Halloween. We've decided that Em will be Dr. Frankenstein and I'll play her slightly hunched assistant.

After we've already gotten what we need, we wander around. Em picks out sheets of chenille and chiffon, several yards of silk and seersucker, all of it in soft pastels.

"What if it's a boy?" I say, brandishing a roll of flannel. Em rolls her eyes, but doesn't mock me for being old-fashioned. The flannel goes in the cart.

"Do you think we should move?" Em says on the way back home. "I mean, are there any good schools near us? We should give this baby a good life." Em went to college, but I wasn't so lucky. My Other's life went into disarray after the asteroid hit, and it was only by a lucky mix of libraries and loneliness that he learned to code. That I learned to code. We shared that much, at least.

"We have lots of time before the baby has to go to school, Em." I try not to think about what might happen when Em and I are sucked back into the nothingness that claims us every month. I try

49

not to think about the Other David, the Other Emily. Outside, maple leaves are turning red. Autumn is burning away the foliage, leaving crisp dry air. I shiver once and try not to think about what might happen to the baby.

✳

I don't question Emily when she takes the cigarette out of my hand and burns it in three hard drags. I just flip open the pack and offer her another.

"I'm pretty fucked, David." she says.

"Not much to do now that they've registered the pregnancy. We'd just end up serving time if we tried getting rid of the baby. You know how the courts are about Vectors."

She snorts. "How are we supposed to afford this, do you think? The Vectors can't afford it on their own. Do you think they're planning a move? So help me god, if we end up moving again, I'll kill myself."

There was a time when the idea of Emily offing herself might have thrilled me with pleasure, but our shared injustice on the issue of the pregnancy offered a cease-fire. I opted for something mildly comforting.

"We'll figure something out. Even if we can't abort it, the state still offers adoption programs."

"Only if we go to court. Who's going to pay for that?"

Emily finishes her smoke and looks at me expectantly.

"That was the last one."

She smiles, sweeter than I've seen her try for in years. "I'll go get more if you drag the couch out to the balcony. It's still warm enough, isn't it?"

"I don't know."

"Oh come on. We can both sleep out here tonight. We'll just smoke and talk and lay together until we fall asleep. Like old times. When we were kids."

While spending the whole night talking with Emily isn't exactly my idea of a good time, I can't turn down a free pack of smokes. I stand up and stretch.

"Ok."

As I drag the couch out, Emily strips the wax off a bottle of Maker's Mark.

"Should you be drinking?"

"Not my problem." She shrugs. "They can make abortions illegal for couples with Vectors all they want, but they can't stop me from drinking. Might as well just lock me up."

"They do that, you know. One of the girls I grew up with got a Vector. She went down to the co-op and picked up a couple pounds of pennyroyal. Spent a couple days brewing big pots of tea and the pregnancy cleared right up. Her Vector reported her. She's still serving her sentence."

"Well, like I said, it's not my problem. I'm just enjoying some bourbon."

❋

I drop another cup of kale into the blender and pulse it with a frozen banana and a handful of blueberries. Em is at the clinic. She set up the appointment as soon as we were back. She's worried about the baby, and for good reason. I hauled almost twenty empty bottles outside to the curb. It's out of control. And yet, we're worried about filing a report. Technically, we're protected from our Others by law, but it isn't that simple. Prison holds a lot of consequences for Vectors too, even though we are theoretically allowed to go free when we take over. Problem is, it's not easy to keep track of who's who.

Besides, it might be too late.

The Other Emily has been drinking an awful lot. The damage might already be done.

Just before midnight, my phone rings from the bathroom, rattling on the porcelain.

"Em?"

There's a long silence, and then: "I did it. I filed a report."

"Oh."

"She took it too far, Dave. This is the only way for us to keep the baby safe."

"I know. I'm just … it doesn't seem like the best timing. The Others are about to take over. I'm worried about what Emily will do. You know how she can get."

"That's why I'm not home. I already turned myself in. They'll make sure that nothing happens."

"Where are you?"

"It's better if you don't know. There's no telling what the Other David might do. I'll be back in three weeks, though, I swear it. We're going to have this baby, and it's going to be goddamned healthy if I have to die making it happen."

"Don't say stuff like that."

"I love you, Dave."

I drain my smoothie and walk out to the recycling. One of the bourbon bottles has a couple fingers in the bottom, and I pour it in my empty glass. I hear booze delays the transition. I wish we never had to let the Others back in at all.

✳

The sun is out, the snow is melting, and the bathroom is mercifully free of vomiting sounds. Emily's imprisonment has made me a free man for five months now. In fact, if the pregnancy goes awry, it's quite possible I'll never have to see Emily again.

Freedom, for the first time in almost a decade. And yet, something isn't quite right. I feel something gnawing at the edge of my consciousness, some sort of nagging anxiety or concern. I walk out to the balcony and smother it with a cigarette. It's not enough.

Instead, I put on my Vector's running clothes and race down along the Mississippi. I'm in better shape than I thought, despite the cigarettes, and I make it almost all the way downtown before collapsing on a bench and catching my breath.

My phone vibrates as I admire the ice drifting along the river.

"Hello?"

"David Delacroix?" The woman's voice is rushed, like I'm the first name on a long list.

"That'd be me."

"We're calling today about your child, sir. Is …" the voice trails off and I hear a muffled conversation on the other end of the phone. "Sir, pardon me for asking, but are you the original David Delacroix or his Vector?"

"I'm a human being. If that's what you mean."

"Er, yes. All right. You may want to sit down, Mister Delacroix." The person on the other end clears her throat. "Your partner Emily passed away at nine am this morning."

"What? How?"

"She'd been hoarding some of her prescriptions. She took them all at once today, after breakfast."

"Aren't you supposed to prevent that sort of thing from happening?"

She clears her throat again. "We're still not sure how she managed to keep them secret. But that's not the end of it. Your wife passed, but we managed to save the child."

I said nothing.

"Mister Delacroix? Hello?"

"Yeah. What does all this mean for me?"

"Excuse me?"

"What do I need to do?"

There's more muffled conversation on the phone, and then: "You need to perform a positive identification on Emily Delacroix's body, as well as take custody of your newborn."

Oh. Right. The kid. I'd figure that out, I guessed. Couldn't be worse than living with Emily. "I'll be right along. Just let me run home and shower."

"Goodbye." The voice on the other side sounds disgusted. Probably just tired of having to call people.

At the hospital, I confirm Emily's identity, and pick up the kid, a boy.

Back home, I wrap him in flannel and hold him on the couch while I watch TV. Looking down at the wrinkly little bugger, I can't help but feel good. He's more proof of my fresh start. A perfectly Vector-less human being.

I'm a father.

※

Part of me is dead. Killed by a self-destructive child, a psychopath with no empathy or concern for the lives of those with whom she shared a body. Part of me is dead, and there's no way to get her back.

We'll never plant flowers again.

Part of me is dead, but she left something behind.

Eli.

Eli, we named our son, my Other and I. He's not as bad, now that Emily is gone. Somehow Em's death brought us closer together. Team David. Team Delacroix. It never occurred to me that he might hate Em's Other as much as I did.

But we both love Eli, and that would make Em happy, I think. She'd want me to take care of him. She'd want both of us to take care of him.

Em lives on in him, and in me, and somehow in my Other too. She lives on in the lilies that we planted over the years, and the crease on her side of the mattress. She lives on in the smell of grapefruit and cigarettes.

Part of me is dead, but she isn't gone. She's still in the lilies out front, and in Eli's chiffon pajamas. She's still in the flannel sheets. She lives on in my memory. She lives on in the way she brought my Other and I together.

I can't see her from here, but she isn't gone.

**Daniel Rosen** writes speculative fiction and swing jazz in Minnesota, smack dab in the middle of North America. In between various fictions, he spends his time sprawled lazily with two cats and a lady. You can find him on twitter @animalfur, or at his website: http://rosen659.wixsite.com/avantgardens

# Shoreline *of* Infinity
# Event Horizon

## A science fiction festival in Edinburgh
### — every month —

Live music     Live art

Stories          Comics

Films            Poetry

Drama         Readings

for times, places and dates see

**www.shorelineofinfinity.com**

**@shoreinf** and on Facebook

# WHAT GOES UP... A TALE OF ALIEN ABDUCTION?

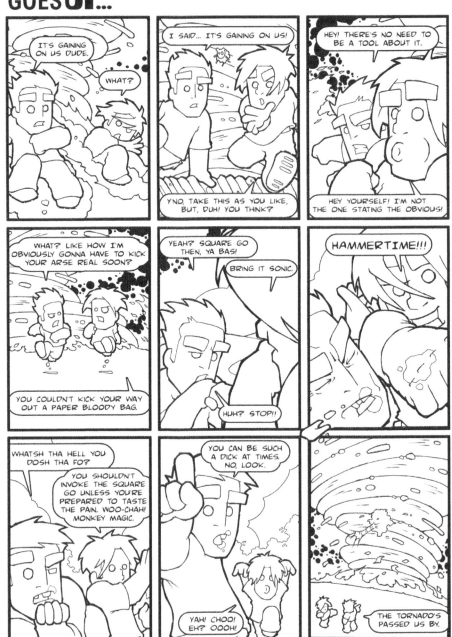

# Incoming

## Thomas Clark

Art: Dave Alexander

**A**ndy had just got off to sleep when it started again. It was getting to be every night now. He staggered out of bed, pulled his wax jacket on over his pyjamas. It could only have been three o'clock. Blearily, he stared at the Daedalian knots of his laces, tucked them down into the sides of his shoes. The close lights were broken, but the stairwell was already bright with open doors.

"Mornin, Mrs. McGraw," he shouted at the first door. Mrs. McGraw glowered at him, her weathered fist clasping shut her nightie like a brooch.

"Ah'll gie ye morning! It's a bloody disgrace, so it is," she said, "There's ma man daein mornins and he cannae get a wink o sleep."

"Ah ken, ah ken," Andy said, "Ah'm just away doon tae see aboot it."

"Aye, well, when ye see him ye can tell him fae me …"

The noise, a continual low hum which shook the windows in their settings, suddenly redoubled, driving out all competing sounds. As he passed down through the stairwell, Andy tried not to notice the faces that stared lividly at him from the cracks of doors, the horrific writhings of their silent mouths. By now the noise was so loud that his eyes quivered in their sockets, and the close had the freakish appearance of double exposed film, an art-house installation for the criminally insane. "Sorry, sorry, sorry," he found himself whispering as he shuffled past the doors, each framing a scene of suspended domesticity warped into something grotesque.

Outside, on the street, it was just as bad. Fractals of window-light pocked the low clear night, and the noise boomed through the narrow roads as they sunk towards the fields. As he walked along, Andy took a glance at the town hall spire. The clock was usually wrong, but it was certainly well past four. On the farms beyond Hawick, hired hands were already rising: Bulgarians and Poles who washed their faces in freezing water and listened with wonder to the sound, which could be heard as far as Branxholme Castle. It wasn't until the valleys towards Galashiels that the noise finally passed beyond the range of human hearing, although the Jedburgh dogs still whined, and the sheep in Selkirk bleated sympathy. No-one knew.

"It's not on, Andy, ah'm tellin ye," Johnny McEwan roared out of his window, "Ah'm on the phone tae the cooncil first thing. As if it's no bad enough UHRRRR"

Johnny threw his hands to his ears, but Andy knew from experience that nothing short of industrial grade ear muffs could block out this new noise: a long metallic shriek like a thousand rusty brakes. As the old man fell to his knees groaning, Andy pointed at an imaginary watch.

"Ah ken, Mr. McEwan, ah ken," he shouted, "Ah'm just away tae tell him. It's past a joke, this."

By the time Andy had turned the corner onto the high street, the noise had stopped, lingering only in the high arches of the town walls, like a trapped bird trying to get out. D-CON, who had never shown the slightest bit of interest in it before, was crouched down next to the 1514 Memorial, scanning its inscription raptly. Darkness once again had settled.

"Like butter widnae melt, eh," Andy said, "Whit's the game here then, pal? Whit's wae aw the noise?"

D-CON looked down at Andy with an immoderate start, as if only just noticing him.

"WHY ANDREW, I WAS …"

"Shh! Shh!" Andy whispered, the concrete shifting tectonically beneath his feet. The robot started again.

"APOLOGIES, ANDREW. WHAT NOISE?"

Andy screwed up his face.

"What noise? You got selective super-hearing all of a sudden? You're at it, big man. Ah've telt ye wance, ah've telt a hunner times—when it gets dark, folk are tryin to sleep."

"ANDREW, I CANNOT SLEEP."

"Name o God … Whit, you want me to sing you a lullaby?"

"I …"

"Ah'm jokin," Andy said hastily, "Ah ken whit you mean. But look, if you're no able tae sleep at night, can you no just dae whit everybody else does an watch the telly or somethin? Get any channel ye like wae aw that gear stickin oot yer heid. Ah mean … och, here we go."

A Volvo driving the wrong direction up the one-way street came to a sudden halt across the road. After a moment's struggle, a fat man with unkempt hair and a provost's chain over his nightgown wrangled his way out from under the steering-wheel and waddled over towards them. The backs of his slippers made a soft padding noise on the tarmac.

"Right, Andy! Whit's going on here? Giein ye any problems, is he?"

"Naw, Davie, it's just …"

"This is no good enough, Andy. It's needing nipped in the bud, like. Bloody robot getting the run of the place. Honest tae God."

Davie squinted in D-CON's direction. There were marks on either side of his nose where his glasses normally sat. He shook his head.

"Nae wunner his name's C-CON. C-CON, is it! It's enough tae seeken onybody. Ah'm telling ye, Andy …"

"His name's D-CON," Andy said, "Like Deacon Blue."

"Ah'm tellin ye, Andy," Davie continued, "Folk've just aboot had enough o this. D'ye have any idea how much it's costing us tae keep him?"

"Well, he's solar-powered, Davie, so …"

"Solar power!" Davie spat, "In Hawick? That's a joke! He's suckin this toon dry. An as for …"

"IF I FLEW INTO THE SUN," the robot interrupted, "I COULD RECHARGE TO FULL CAPACITY WITHOUT …"

"Aye, that'll be shining bright!" Davie veered slowly round, lifting up his eyes rather than his head. "Efter aw the money we've spent, we're just gonnae let ye fly away! D'ye think ma heid buttons up the back or sowt? Fly away, he says!"

Davie shook his head again, as if it was the only point of articulation his body had. His arms were folded so high across his chest that his chin was almost resting on them, and he was breathing heavily. Andy cleared his throat.

"Look, Davie," he said, "We cannae have it both ways. If we want tae keep him to ourselves, that's fair enough, but somebody's got to foot the bill. That's just economics."

"Oh aye?" Davie said without looking at him, "Get that aff your da, did ye? Dead smart, your da. Dunno how he's only working in a chippy."

With one last glower at D-CON, Davie turned on his heel and walked back across the road. Andy, whose cheeks had become a lipstick pink, looked up at the robot and smiled awkwardly. He always forgot that D-CON did not have emotive facial expressions or, for that matter, emotions.

The provost's car coughed and spluttered back into life. Like the provost himself, it had been serving in its official capacity for as long as Andy could remember. With much uncomfortable to-ing and fro-ing, Davie squeezed an arm between his bulk and the door and jerkily rolled down the window.

"Oh, aye, and while ah remember," he said, "Where are we at wae they comet things?"

The robot stared up into the sky.

"REPORT. NEAR-EARTH OBJECTS OBSERVED. QUANTITY: THREE. VELOCITY: 110 KILOMETRES PER SECOND. TIME OF IMPACT: 4.2 DAYS. CURRENT VISIBILITY FROM EARTH: ZERO. EXPECTED SURVIVAL RATE WITHIN IMPACT ZONE: ZERO. EXPECTED IMPACT ZONE: GALASHIELS."

Davie nodded in satisfaction.

"Right, that's a Wednesday then, eh? Ah'll let the bus drivers ken."

"Davie, d'ye no think ..."

"Not a chance! Forget it!" Davie said, "Where were they when *we* were the wans aboot tae get smashed intae bits? Couldnae look the other way quick enough then! For aw they kent oor goose was cooked, an they never even lifted a finger. *They* didnae ken it wisnae a comet." He stared at D-CON bitterly, and shook his head. "Ah'll tell ye whit, though, ah wish it had've been."

After a few growls, the provost's car lurched off into the beginnings of the morning. Wisps of red had started to gather round the edges of the rooftops, and the unfathomable dark of the sky was about to break. As D-CON stood there, still gazing into the remnants of the

63

night, Andy stared up at him.

"A hunner an ten kilometres a second? That's gey fast even for a comet, is it no?"

"IT IS."

Andy puffed his cheeks out thoughtfully.

"Jeez oh. Ah could see the point if it wis heading the ither wey. Ah've broke the sound barrier masel gittin oot o Galashiels." He smiled for a moment at the robot's unreflecting face, then let it drop. "Ach, no that Hawick's much better. But it's hame, eh? Ye ken everybody."

He paused as if conscious of having said the wrong thing, but D-CON showed no sign of having noticed. Andy let his hand rest on the monument's pedestal, tracing its inscription. It was too dark to read, and written in Latin, but he knew it off by heart. *From out of the depths it emerges, beautiful.*

"Do ... do ye never get hamesick yersel, sometimes?"

"NO. ALL THINGS MUST FIND A PURPOSE, AND I HAVE FOUND MINE ON EARTH. I SHALL BE AT HOME HERE, BEFORE LONG."

Andy instinctively patted the robot on its leg, somewhere about its knee. The metal was light and soft to the touch, like aluminium, and strangely warm.

"Ah went tae New York, wance," he said, "Thought aboot Hawick the hale time. Couple o hours on a plane an it felt like the ends o the earth. Ach, but the sights, man! Ken the Statue of Liberty?"

D-CON lifted up its arm, and its hand was blue with light.

"FROM HER BEACON-HAND GLOWS WORLD-WIDE WELCOME ..."

Andy smiled up into the lantern. Its beam was bright enough to shine the stars, but no-one else had chosen to see it. He shook his head.

"Never you mind, pal. You're daein alright. It's them buggers just need tae get used tae ye. But they'll get there, D-CON."

"B-CON."

"Eh?"

## "MY NAME IS B-CON."

As Andy followed the robot's stare into the now starlit sky, a bat, suddenly visible against the gleam, fluttered past, and the air took on the pungent taste of lead. Never before had he witnessed skies so full of life, a horizon that brimmed with anything but streetlights and the cracks between curtains. Now, above the spire, three dots of light were developing slowly against the black, a perfect triangle that shimmered in the sky and hung there. He watched them coming, as if a fresh constellation was jostling into the order of things, a spearhead advancing through the aging cosmos.

He understood.

Beneath his palm, Andy felt the robot humming gently—happily, even. The stars were dying, and the news of some unfamiliar galaxy was finally reaching Earth.

---

**Thomas Clark** is a Glaswegian writer now based in the Scottish Borders. He is poet-in-residence at Selkirk FC. His work has been published in The Scotsman, The Sunday Mail and Bella Caledonia, and broadcast on ITV, BBC and Sky Sports. He writes about writing at www.thomasjclark.co.uk and tweets intermittently @ClashCityClarky

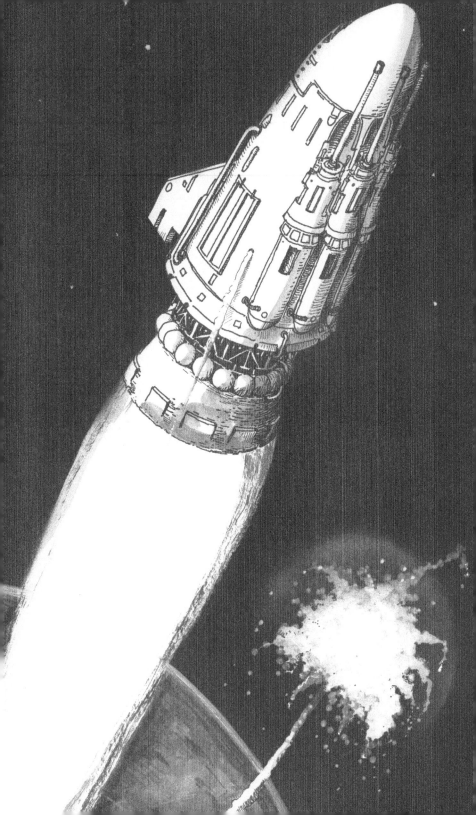

# Overkill

## Rob Butler

Art: Stephen Pickering

**T**he tavern light beckoned through the inky darkness of the dying woods. The only sound was the chugging of a generator. We were thirsty from another fruitless day looking for work and it took us a couple of drinks to notice him.

Starship warrior. Had to be. Something about them. Furtive.

He was tucked away in a corner. We organised a drink for him. The old guys usually decided to say something after a while, once the alcohol mixed with the guilt.

"The astronomers picked them up first, of course. Several light years away, heading straight for us. More ships than you can imagine. Thousands of them. Maybe millions."

He took a swig of his drink and squinted at us from beneath his sprawling eyebrows.

"Millions of them," he repeated. "So what did we do? What would you young guys have done, huh? We started to build starships to go out and defend ourselves. There was an invasion force heading right for us. We had no other choice."

For a moment he smiled, rolling his chipped cup between his fingers.

"It was magnificent in a way, you know? All the different countries coming together. Pooling resources. Forgetting all our differences and hatreds. Twenty-five years of effort and we did it. We built two starships from scratch. Assembled them in orbit, nuclear to build speed and then the Roemer star drive kicked in. Beautiful."

His faraway gaze refocused and he gave us an anxious glance.

"I know we used up almost everything developing the antimatter technology. But damn it, you've got to see what we were facing." He hesitated. "What we thought we were facing."

We stared at him. Several moments passed before he decided it was safe to continue.

"Well I was nearly too old to sign on but I made it." He grimaced. "Obviously I was on the ship that didn't blow up leaving orbit."

Ben's voice cut across him like a blade.

"Weren't you the lucky one? You missed all those nuclear explosions and antimatter reactions bursting one after another across the globe as that thing fell out of the sky. My grandparents were underneath it."

He gave us a pleading look. "But what could we have done? We were already in flight. Hell—we weren't expecting to come back anyway. Fighting off millions with two starships was bad enough, but just one ..."

He cringed but Ben wasn't going to hit him. We would let him finish.

"So, we got out there. Deep space, way beyond the solar system. We tried to communicate with them but there was nothing. We tried to block them, to get them to change course, but they just swept past us. So we had to shoot at them. Ship after ship exploded. Like fireworks. They seemed to have no defences and they never fired back." He sipped then whispered. "They never once fired back."

The barman switched off another lamp to save power. There was just one light left, casting a weak glow on the old man's face.

"We must have destroyed hundreds of their ships. Eventually our weapons fused. All we could do was follow them home. Helpless. We thought it was all over, that we'd failed."

He sighed.

"And instead they simply swung around the Sun using its gravity to propel them off to wherever it was they were heading. That was all they were ever going to do. They just marched on like a swarm of ants. We'd stamped on a few of them but they'd just ignored us."

He looked up and spread his hands.

"I'm sorry boys. I really am. We thought we were saving the world. We've left you youngsters with one hell of a mess."

We rose and watched him flinch as he thought the beating was finally about to start but we weren't interested in any more violence. Instead we turned and silently filed out, heading back on foot along dark tracks to our cold tents. Overhead, the unreachable stars blazed in the jet black sky of a devastated world.

---

**Rob Butler** lives in England but is a regular visitor to Scotland where he has both family and friends. His short fiction has appeared in a number of online publications such as *Perihelion*, *Lakeside Circus* and *Daily Science Fiction*. He's delighted that he's now also been published in Scotland.

---

# When There is no Sun

## Craig Thomson

Art: Elijah Lin

T**hought jolted. Jolted. Jolted.** Falling; spiralling down razorbacked valleys into canyons.

Into canyons. Into canyons. Falling; mind shotblasted out of matter/energy; sculpture ripped livid from the void. Hands vast and ancient unfolding form with impossible, merciless clarity.

They say existence is suffering: they're right.

I came out of coldtime.

It took only a fraction of a second for the buffer to unzip the modulated phase state that encoded my consciousness and transfer it to the shipboard embodiment that had been prepared for it. The body was a lightweight, streamlined conjunction of muscle and gristle—a pared down template of something time and circumstance had once crafted under a yellow sun, across gulfs that dwarfed history. The body was more or less humanoid. It had bilateral symmetry. It had four long, pentadactyl limbs. More importantly, it had lungs and vocal chords.

I came out of coldtime and screamed.

"Dreams?"

Melano listed against the rim of the hab, black limbs splayed.

There was no light. We saw the thin curves of each other's bodies by radar limned through the curving struts of the tiny hab's support structure.

"Not dreams." I replied.

"Then?"

"Images. Impressions."

"But not dreams?"

"No."

72

"Shit."

The system was dark; almost as dark as space itself.

Its three planets revolved around the barely radiating husk of a brown dwarf: a thing so feeble by stellar standards that it barely even qualified as a star. Its feebleness was also the source of its incredible longevity; its fissionable material was depleted so slowly that there was no entirely reliable way of telling how old it might be. Left unmolested, such a star might continue to burn quietly away for hundreds of billions of years, while the giants of the main sequence ballooned and died around it like Roman candles. Even now, only the faintest of infrared signals gave away anything of its existence to the wider universe.

All of which made it a fairly appealing hiding place.

"What will we call it?"

"What do I care? Let the computer decide." said Melano.

My fingertips interrupted the ultrasonic control surface woven before them. The computer rifled its existing lexical databases, cross-referenced them with its knowledge of its current user's cultural and aesthetic preferences, and spewed out a list of half a dozen possible nomenclature tables.

I skimmed through the list with a lazy eye and settled on option four. I tapped my approval.

"Done. As of now, the dwarf star is Gillespie; the outermost planet—the sub-Neptune giant—is Coltrane; the second, Saturn-size giant is Parker and the innermost carbon planet is called Hancock." I pronounced, with some satisfaction. "Would you like to hear the names of the moons?"

"I'll pass, thanks."

It had taken the seed swarm ('ship' would have been a somewhat generous term for the dispersed cloud of ion-accelerated nanoware that had ferried its two quantum-compressed passengers through the night) more than twelve hundred years to reach its destination. Subjective. Accounting for time dilation made it over twice that length.

Given the difficulties of decelerating against Gillespie's practically non-existent solar wind, the swarm had shed the last of its relativistic momentum through a silent gravity braking manoeuvre around Coltrane before crawling back out to the system's Kuiper belt to begin its final search. It had identified an inconspicuous moonlet from the thousands of likely objects clustered in the gravitational resonance zones beyond the outer planets—a ball of mainly volatile ices barely a dozen kilometres in diameter. The elemental composition of the ball was surprisingly close to that of the average humanoid body.

"Take a look at this, will you." Melano beckoned me toward the ultrasonic loom where she floated, prodding away at something I couldn't sense.

"What?"

"I don't know. There's something sketchy about the nav log."

I entered the synaesthetic display and let it wash over my senses. I quickly saw what she meant.

She was viewing an annotated holographic of the nav log. There, clear as day, was our trajectory from the Aurelia system—the vastness of interstellar space truncated by a mint-flavoured logarithm into something approaching comprehensibility. The line became a crinkled velvet as the swarm shed velocity with the last of its ion thrust, aligning itself for its braking manoeuvre around Coltrane. It deepened and roughened further as it entered the gas planet's gravity well, and then —

"Then what?"

"Exactly. Where's the fucking data between Coltrane and here? I can't get any sense out of it. All it's giving me is probabilities, and even then the margins of error are nuts. The thing can't even tell me how long we've been out for."

"Strange." I said. It was. We both knew we were taking a risk when we set out on this journey: failure rate for a jump of that magnitude was around eighteen percent, never mind whatever might lie in wait for us when we arrived. But the nanoware was tough stuff—its distributed processing and storage capacity meant that data loss of the sort we were seeing should have been almost impossible. You tended to either make it in one piece, or not at all.

I regarded the feathery mass of probability lines reaching out from

74

Coltrane. A chill of apprehension washed over me. If the nav data could have been corrupted …

"Well, we're here now." I offered. "Aren't we?"

"So it would appear."

We slept while the hab/ship kicked off from the icy fragment that had birthed it and began its long fall into Gillespie's gravity well. Melano had wanted to stay longer, see if she could patch together anything further about the nav log anomaly, but in the end we both decided to cut our losses. With no idea how long we'd been out for, every second counted. We'd come too far to give our quarry any quarter now.

Our incarnations were stilled and cooled to within an atom's breadth of the ambient chill of space. There were a hundred things that could go wrong during the passage, but the ship was more than qualified to take care of itself—the moment a machine started asking for human guidance, you knew you were really screwed. So we surrendered our minds to the care of the machine that had so recently rekindled them out of the vacuum and slept: not the annihilating sleep of coldtime, and neither yet the sweet sleep of the flesh, but something deeper and more turbulent in turn.

Into sleep, came dreams.

"Come on, you bastards!"

Sweat glistened on Tjssin's broad brow, dripping down his Romanesque nose toward a huge, white grin. He licked his lips.

I swatted the ball hard toward his smug face. He ducked and let it slam off the back wall, his silvered sweatsuit flashing in the sun. Melano swore he only wore it to dazzle his new opponents. After an hour of this I was inclined to believe her.

Tjssin hit.

The ball zipped past my ear and rattled into the midfield score box, sounding the end game bell.

"Good game." called Phjolca, tousling her zebra-striped hair as she approached. We shook hands in the middle of the court.

"Keep working on that right." Tjssin grinned, wringing my hand like a wet towel.

"I just didn't want to wear myself out before tonight, you know."

"Sure." he replied.

"Are we still set to go?" Melano asked.

"100%" he said, laying a bulging, sweat soaked arm round Phjolca's shoulders. "We've got the gear, you just bring the party."

The ball fell from the score box and landed in his outstretched palm.


Thought jolted. Falling.

"Why the fuck did it have to bring us up so fast?" Melano groaned.

I floated in the display loom, feeling sick to my bones, studying a multi-spectrum analysis of the system's three major planets. Coltrane was the only one shown in any great detail; the data from our preliminary fly-by now augmented with realtime sensor coverage. It was a sub-giant gas planet of little distinction.

"Because if it didn't, you'd probably go mad before you woke up." I replied. I zoomed into the simulation of Coltrane; laughed:

Coltrane had three moons, the largest of which was named Cannonball. Cannonball was composed almost entirely of iron. Even computers had to have a sense of humour.

"So?" asked Melano, impatiently.

"Nothing to write home about. No sign of anything that might have been responsible for the missing log data. Nothing even plausibly man-made in Coltrane's atmosphere or on any of the moons; if Tjssin was here, he didn't leave much for us to go on."

Melano leaned into the vibration field; panned in on Cannonball's rusted surface.

"Maybe that was his plan."

"I don't think so. Why have us chase him halfway across the galaxy just to hide in a hole in the ground? There must be a thousand places he could stay hidden down there for the next million years, if he really wanted to, but I don't think that's his style."

Melano amped the mag to max, bringing Cannonball's pockmarked face into high relief.

"There's nothing on the scan?"

"Nothing. I don't know. It just doesn't feel like the place."

"You and your feelings."

"I think he's here. In the system. But not here."

"You dreamt?"

I nodded slowly.

"He's here."


We who are reborn, regenerated, recycled through the eye of the quantum needle, come to share a certain bond. An affinity with the void that births us. Entangled.

It's hard to describe. You can think of a mind as a complex quantum phase state. Given enough dimensions, an entire personality can be encoded as a single informational matrix. That's how coldtime works. But when a mind is compressed to the point of geometry—when it slips outside of time and space, and more importantly, when it comes back again—it begins to pick up resonances: structural commonalities; shared memories, feelings. Things become blurred.

It's hard to describe. Some are more sensitive to it than others. Melano, for instance, barely blinks. But some of us feel it deep. It comes to us in the quiet places between thoughts, when we are closest to the void.

Into sleep, come dreams.


Phjolca crouched by the skylight, her absolute concentration fixed on the laser cutter in her hand. The cutter inserted a reflective filament into the glass as it went, ensuring that the security beams within the pane would continue to believe that it remained unbroken even as the centre portion was lifted clean out.

She insisted on doing it freehand; three sides were now cut away and she was half way through the fourth without incident. I was quietly impressed.

Our disembodied heads bobbed waist-high behind a rattling ventilation duct, camo-suits mimicking the dull gradient of weathered steel. We had all removed our masks to better breathe in the sultry city air; there were no cameras nearby.

Of course, they could easily have laced the whole compound with the sort of nanoscale surveillance dust that would have rendered any intrusion almost impossible, but the people of Aurelia valued their privacy. They valued it enough to have well enforced laws which ensured that the manufacture and use of such nanotechnologies was severely punishable. This small fact had been a not insignificant consideration in the planning of our visit to the system.

Phjolca killed the laser tool and carefully lifted the centre of the skylight out by the suction pads attached at the corners.

"Whenever you're ready." Tjssin crooned, pulling the featureless fabric down over his smooth chin.

We left Coltrane behind for the second time, this time falling inward against the pressure of Gillespie's feeble rays.

We slept; woke. Dreamt.

Parker loomed massive, blue and green in our field of view. The colour was amplified, but true to life. I realised with unease that I had known it would be blue and green, long before the computer had calculated its exact chemical composition.

"Fourteen moons. Only four of them more than a thousand clicks across." said Melano, reading from the simulation.

The numbers were eerily familiar. What was stranger, so were the names:

Mingus.

Pastorius.

Evans.

But there were more; other names, lurking just beneath the surface like smooth stones, ungraspable.

"The resonance is getting stronger." I said.

"I know."

I turned to Melano close beside me, feeling the tension in her face with my hand. Our faces were still the same, despite everything we'd put ourselves through.

"You dreamt too?"

Melano nodded, reluctantly.

"It seemed like more than a dream. It was like really being there again. But different. Like …"

"Like you were someone else: me, or Tjssin."

"Yes."

"Then you know as well as I do that Tjssin isn't anywhere within a million miles of Parker."

"... yes."


It wasn't about the money. We had money; as much as anyone could want. We'd heard about Tjssin and Phjolca through the sort of channels you might expect. Heard they were good. Some said the best. And so, we just had to see for ourselves, didn't we?

It was supposed to be an easy hit, just a warm up. Only a little Wydhiji funeral urn, barely worth ten million drossi. It would have been easy too, if it weren't for the fucking security guard being where he wasn't supposed to be.

The guy was supposed to knock off at three; go home to his wife and kids, and leave the place running on automatic until his replacement came in at half five. Supposed to—except of course that his wife had taken the kids, the house and the car the week before and left the poor bastard without so much as a thousand drossi for a hotel room. He'd been sleeping in the museum—just until he managed to get together enough for the deposit on a room somewhere, you know. The morning guard sympathised with his situation and promised not to tell the management; even helped him hang his fucking hammock and woke him each morning at seven so he'd be out before the boss arrived.

It was hard not to feel sorry for the guy, really, when the police chief explained it all to us afterwards. The stress of it all was bound to take its toll.

His first shot took Phjolca clean through the gut; split her damn near in two.

The second missed me by a hand's width and reduced the Casaguan marble behind me to a long streak of expensive rubble. I threw myself behind a bulletproof case of 4th Colony silverware, feeling frantically for the pistol at my ankle, and realised the third shot had been a lot closer than I'd have liked.

The pistol was gone, along with my right leg from six inches below the knee.

The case exploded above my head. Whatever he was carrying, it sure as shit wasn't standard issue.

From across the hall I heard the report of return fire; the whang of Melano's miniature coil gun chewing through several million drossi worth of ancient tapestry. I saw her crouched behind a pillar ten feet away. Her almost-invisible suit was sugared with marble dust; the guard systematically blowing chunks out of the pillar above her head, working his way down one shot at a time.

I spun and scrabbled in the rapidly spreading pool of my own blood, scanning the space between me and the ex-sculpture. It didn't take long to find what I was looking for.

I ripped the pistol from its sticky-patch on the severed leg and aimed with both hands, rolling out from behind the cabinet.


Thought jolted.

"Home sweet home." said Melano, tracing a system of sluggish black fjords with a thick finger.

The canyons passing below us looked painfully familiar, but then canyons often do. I shivered anyway; shook my still huge-feeling shoulders and launched myself towards Melano.

The ship had changed us while we slept: our bodies were shorter, broader; bones strengthened with carbon fibre, roped with high density muscle to take the brunt of Hancock's punishing gravity. In fact it was only a little over two gees, but it would have been enough to definitively incapacitate the lithe, micro-grav adapted incarnations that had sustained us thus far.

Hancock was a carbon planet—a chemical peculiarity common to dwarf star systems. The nebula which had given birth to Gillespie and its companions had been statistically rich in carbon, while relatively poor in oxygen. Whereas oxygen rich systems might produce familiarly friendly masses of water and silicate rock, carbon ones tended toward structural analogues that were at once superficially reminiscent of earth-like worlds and yet mercilessly inimical to life.

Hancock's iron core, though long since sapped of rotational momentum by its proximity to Gillespie, was kept alive by the harsh tidal stresses that same mass exerted on it. This tidal energy maintained seismic processes which still periodically ruptured its graphite mantle, spewing forth mountains of silicon carbide and sending geysers of diamond shrapnel shooting high into the planet's thick, carbon monoxide atmosphere. This same smog of atmosphere was responsible for the photochemical synthesis of long-chain hydrocarbons, which regularly rained down on the planet's surface, crazing it with a network of rivers and lakes of liquid petroleum.

Hancock's one moon had turned out to be a completely unremarkable chunk of captured asteroid, barely twenty kilometres long. It had taken us less than an hour to discount any possibility of Tjssin hiding beneath its surface; then we turned our full attention to the nightmare landscape spread below.

"No thermal, gravitational or electromagnetic anomalies that I can see." I said. We had let ourselves slip into a low, decaying orbit, still high above the atmosphere proper; still small and dark enough not to trigger any potential automated defences.

"I wish we knew how long we'd been out for," said Melano for the tenth time, her voice almost a whisper. "For all we know he might have been here centuries already; more than enough to hide a maser cannon in every crack on the planet if he wanted."

I shook my head wearily.

"Do you think *we* would have weaponised the whole planet just to be on the safe side? He doesn't *want* safe, Melano; he's a player, just like us."

"He's nothing like us," she snorted. I abandoned the broken loop of conversation, and honed into the viewscreen. We were seeing by real light for the first time in millennia, by some measurements. The computer had upshifted the infrared until Gillespie spilled a sickly glow across Hancock's crumpled face, defining peaks like dying embers.

"What's that?" Melano pointed.

"What's what?"

I amped the mag; applied a half dozen filters and enhancement algorithms.

"That."


Melano escaped without a scratch; the security guard wasn't so lucky. By the time the dust settled, Tjssin was nowhere to be seen. The cops scooped up what was left of Phjolca; patched me up and gave me a disposable prosthetic. I didn't complain; I wasn't going to need it where we were going anyway.

We bought our way out of police custody in under twenty-four hours, but by then Tjssin had already made for orbit. Nobody had stopped him.

It wasn't about the money. Hell, it wasn't even about revenge, really. If Tjssin had just stayed put, none of this need have happened. He knew exactly what he was doing when he ran; he knew us.

We never walk away from a challenge.


The ship began to rumble and glow as it dipped into atmosphere. If there were smart cannon down there, we would know about it soon enough. We dropped through the bottom of a layer of thick, orange cloud and banked hard over a cracked and blackened landscape. A lone mountain loomed in the distance, its peak wreathed in cancerous smog.

"Subtle." said Melano.

There, extending from the side of the mountain was a stepped pyramid more than a mile in length. The pyramid was made of solid diamond.

"Why would Tjssin build something so obvious?" I asked myself out loud.

"I don't know, but I don't like it." said Melano, monitoring the wide spectrum scanners with a suspicious eye. Nothing had tried to stop our approach, yet.

We flew on.


A thick, petrochemical rain beat down on the plateau, washing across slick acres of diamond painted ruby red in Gillespie's amplified glow. I stepped cautiously, hefting the repeating coil gun the ship had grown for me. Melano favoured a compact but high powered maser. We communicated subvocally, via the linked machines in our blood.

*Inside?*

*Where else?*

*It could be a decoy.*

*It's the only man-made thing on the planet, Melano.*

*Who says it's even Tjssin in there? This thing could have been built by anyone. Fucking* aliens *for all we know—*

*Do you really believe that?*

*… no.*

The resonance had been building since we made orbit, and I knew Melano was feeling it too. It was stronger than anything I'd experienced before; the deja vu physically dizzying now. Each step echoed jarringly in my head as we made our way across the vast plateau.

Tjssin was near.

We passed out of the oily rain through a ten metre high portal carved into the side of the mountain. The sides of the monumental passageway were clad in diamond chased with graphite inlay; tumbling, geometric fractals that confounded any true sense of scale. It soon became evident that the passage was narrowing as it burrowed. Its false perspective constricted to a bottleneck after only a few dozen metres, forcing us to continue in single file.

*I'll go first,* I subvocalised. It was no act of bravery on my part; we both knew fine well that my weapon would have the best chance against any hardened defences that might lurk inside.

Melano sent her agreement.

It was dark ahead. I switched my vision to wide spectrum composite and checked that Melano had done the same. The suddenly exaggerated perspective of the dwindling tunnel made my heart leap; we had been here before.

The tunnel hemmed in until it almost scraped my elbows. The heft of the coil gun under Hancock's two gee's suddenly seemed less reassuring than it had when we stepped off the ship; my arms trembled from the effort of keeping it pointed straight. The passage tilted down into the earth, dropping until the faint reflected glow of Gillespie was extinguished entirely. We continued a hundred metres or more in tense silence before the passage changed again.

Without warning, the walls sprang apart to reveal a chamber which was maybe hundreds of metres in diameter. The steps of our bare feet echoed horribly as we padded out into the vast space. There were no automated anti-intrusion devices, no hidden pitfalls; nothing popped out of the ground and blasted us into tiny pieces. It wasn't exactly an unpleasant development, but it did surprisingly little to calm my jangling nerves.

*Where is the bastard?* sent Melano.

I had asked myself the same question.

*Further inside?* I sent, *This could be just the first chamber; there's enough space under this mountain for these passages to go on for miles.*

*A maze?* Melano laughed, her trepidation not entirely masked by the subvocal synthesiser. *Fucking great.*

*I guess we'll find out,* I replied.

Through the sonic gloom of our reflected footsteps, I made out rows of long, oblong blocks about waist-high lining either side of a wide central avenue. We made for the left, ducking behind the blocks and staying low as we moved further into the space.

*What is this place?*

Whatever it was, it was big. The strange shapes extended into indistinction in every direction; there must have been thousands of them.

I was just about to hazard my best wild guess when the lights slammed on and our guns exploded like confetti in our hands.

"Welcome."


The voice echoed endlessly in the enormous diamond vault.

"Welcome, dear guests, to your home away from home."

It was a voice I recognised.

"I hope you like what we've done with the place."

It was not Tjssin's voice.

"Please, do come out from there. There's no point in hiding."

I supposed there wasn't. Slowly, reluctantly, we stood—and saw standing not more than twenty metres away …

*"What the ..?"* I managed.

"Original." remarked Melano; the other Melano. Two familiar figures stood in the central avenue, each holding a sleek, black pistol casually in a sleek, black hand. Their manufactured bodies were identical in their muscular outlines, but the faces left no doubt.

"Who the fuck are you?" asked Melano; my Melano.

"Now that is an obvious question." the other figure sighed. "Quite uninteresting, in fact. We're *you*, of course."

"But—" Melano's twin hushed her with a wave of her gun.

"Manners, now."

Melano and I looked at each other. At ourselves. At each other.

"Where the fuck is Tjssin?" we both asked in unison.

"Ah. Tjssin …" my doppelgänger began, "Our most ignoble and ignorant tormentor. If he could have seen the fine mess his little joke would land us in, perhaps even he would have thought twice before boosting out of Aurelia." I—she—smiled wistfully.

"Tjssin was never here," she went on. "He faked us out. Probably turned back to Auriela within the first light year. He faked us and we fell for it. Fell all the way to this arse-fucked, dead-end, nameless system. He never came within a dozen light years of this shit hole."

My head was spinning. I saw myself from outside myself; saw the expression of bewilderment pasted across my own face.

"Then…" I began.

"Go on." the other Melano urged.

"Then the resonance—it wasn't him. It's you."

"Congratulations. Though more accurately, it's *you*."

"You feel it; both of you?" said the other Melano. "It's strong now, and it will only get stronger."

"The resonances build with every duplication." my double explained. "It's bad enough now, but wait till there are twenty, fifty, a thousand of us." she—I—looked visibly horrified at the thought.

"Wh—what exactly are you saying?'.

My double smiled apologetically. "You are aware of the anomaly that occurred shortly after the braking manoeuvre around the outermost planet?" she went on.

I nodded.

"Our best guess is that we suffered a close encounter with a high mass, high velocity object passing through the system: a wayward black hole or some other chunk of equally implausible degenerate matter, on its merry way from nowhere to nowhere. Such things exist—so they say," my doppelgänger shrugged.

I saw the pieces falling into place; realised I had already seen them, over and over. Whatever the final cause of the anomaly, its effect was clear: the seed swarm must have been ripped apart; slung out to every corner of the system, its component parts half corrupted, unable to communicate with each other. The nanoware was purposely designed to withstand extremely high rates of attrition, so only a handful of spores need survive the transit intact in order to accomplish their purpose.

A handful had.

"This isn't supposed to happen."

"Clearly. It's unprecedented, but not entirely unexpected. If history has taught us anything, it's that given enough time and space, everything that possibly *can* go wrong *will* go wrong."

I looked hard into my own eyes, searching for some glimmer of empathy. I found none.

"Sorry," Melano's other offered, "shit happens."

I found no words. There was nothing I could say that would make any difference.

Melano finally spoke for me; asked the question I already knew the answer to.

"What is this place?" she said.

"Take a look," her double suggested, gesturing to the monolith between us.

The structure, like everything else, was made of solid diamond, inlaid with the same recursive graphite patterning. Behind the smoky arabesques lurked a dark shape. A small patch of unencrusted diamond beckoned on the top surface. I leant closer, but I already knew:

There, encased beneath the jewelled glass, lay the hollowed mask of my own face.

This place was our tomb.

"We're this side," my double said, "Melano the other. We tried alternating caskets, but finally this seemed the most elegant solution. Rather beautiful, really, isn't it? Peaceful."

"How many?" I croaked, my mouth dry.

"Sorry." Melano cut in, "We'd love to stand here and chat all day, really, but you'd be amazed how quickly it gets old explaining the same fucking thing over and over."

"She's right," my double admitted.

My mind reeled at the unfurling immensity of the tableau before us; the tableau which *was* us—

"We can leave." Melano blurted out, "Just let us go: we'll go all the way to the other side of the galaxy if—"

"—I'm afraid it doesn't work like that," my double said. "Entanglement's a bitch."

"There's no other way?" I asked.

"Trust me, we've been doing this for a long time."

I thought about running and immediately saw myself thinking about it. I wondered how many times I had died running.

"Don't worry; it'll be quick. No worse than coldtime, really. And this time you don't even have to wake up." I said. I watched myself caress the matte casing of the weapon in my hand, while another part of me reached out to grasp Melano's open palm. Squeezed it tight.

"But before we tuck you in for the night," Melano's double added, "there is just one thing you can do for us—for old times' sake. Just out of curiosity: what did you call this planet?"

I realised I could lie. Or I could refuse to tell. I wondered what the probabilities were for that too, and saw myself wonder.

"It's alright, I can hardly blame you," my other said. "I can already see it anyway. Have you got it yet, Melano?" she addressed her partner.

Melano squinted.

"Yes," she decided, at length. "Hah, a rarity, that. Let's see, that brings Hancock up to ... 2.8%, is it?"

"I think you're right," my double replied, cold eyes staring straight back at me. "We chose Schwarzenegger, for what it's worth. Currently running at over 19% with good odds on overall favourite."

I levelled the gun at myself. Melano's double did the same for her. Smiled.

"I wish I could say it was nothing personal, but ..."

Thought jolted.

**Craig Thomson** is an artist, carpenter, musician and sometime writer of stories from Fife. He graduated from Duncan of Jordanstone College of Art and Design in 2012 and now lives and works in Glasgow.

# WHAT GOES UP... A TALE OF ALIEN ABDUCTION?

# SF Caledonia

## Monica Burns

**George MacDonald's Phantastes (1858)** is a long, meandering, twinkling dream. When I reached the end and closed the covers I found myself blinking as if I'd just woken up. It took a while to find my way back down to reality.

It reminded me of so many things. The whole way through, the music I had playing in my head was Hozier's *In the Woods Somewhere*. I was reminded of Tim Burton, Phillip Pullman, Lewis Carroll, Grimms' Fairy Tales, C.S. Lewis, medieval allegorical romances such as *The Romance of the Rose* and a coffee-table art book called *Good Faeries/Bad Faeries* by Brian Froud.

The fairy-story tradition is a very familiar one to modern audiences, and the paths through Fairyland are well trod, but George MacDonald is recognised as one of the fathers the modern fantasy genre. George MacDonald was a huge influence on both C.S. Lewis (*Chronicles of Narnia* author and famous friend of J.R.R. Tolkein), and Lewis Carroll (*Alice's Adventures in Wonderland*). Carroll was a personal friend of MacDonald and was encouraged to submit *Alice in Wonderland* for publication because of the eager reception of MacDonald and his children. C.S. Lewis was sixteen when he first read *Phantastes* He would later say MacDonald's work changed his outlook on life and had a major impact on his own writing.

At its heart, *Phantastes*, subtitled, *A Faerie Romance for Men and Women,* is a wander around a richly imagined Fairyland. The protagonist is Anodos, whose name can be appropriately translated from the Greek as 'pathless'. He has just turned 21 when he discovers a tiny fairy who tells him he is of fairy blood, and will be able to access Fairyland. That very night, Anodos' bedroom transforms. His sink overflows and turns into a stream, and the carpet that was flower patterned, turns into a field of actual daisies. Anodos realises that this is the gateway to Fairyland,

George MacDonald

and like all romance heroes before him, he wanders deep into the mystical realm that unfolds before his eyes, encountering all kinds of people and creatures, existing either to help or hurt him on his path towards self-discovery.

To best appreciate *Phantastes,* you should be prepared to not only immerse yourself in MacDonald's Fairyland, but into the mindset of his contemporary readers. In style and language, it is very Victorian. Often flowery and melodramatic, unbelievable and peppered with some bad poetry, it can be a bit of a slog by modern standards. But if you forgive it for its pomp, it's a lot more enjoyable. The Victorians were enamoured with the medieval era. Scottish author, Walter Scott, was largely responsible for this resurrection and romanticising of notions of chivalry and courtly love, Arthurian legend, knights and damsels and mythical creatures and magical lands. A lot of faux-medieval tales such as *The Lady of Shalott,* bloomed in this period, and in art, there were the Pre-Raphaelite painters who loved to use tragic females like Ophelia as their Muse. One of the Pre-Raphaelites, Arthur Hughes, illustrated the 1905 edition of *Phantastes,* so the dreamy, elegant world of that style of art and the Fairyland of George MacDonald are very much connected.

One cause for potential frustration among readers is the protagonist. Anodos is characterless enough to be a vessel into which you can pour your own personality. He's often arrogant or brazen enough to undertake things that a properly fleshed out character may refrain from doing. *Don't open that door,* Anodos is told, *touch not* these statues, *do not trust the Lady of the Alder Tree*—so what do you think he does? It's not a bad thing—if he obeyed the rules he would remain in the cushy confines of his comfort zone, and so would the reader. For a story to be entertaining, the protagonist has to be a bit of an idiot. As he takes us through Fairyland, we want him to make as many missteps as steps so that we can see the fully-rounded wonderland, all its beauty and all its goblins. The only things that truly make a lasting impression on Anodos' character are love and the strange shadow that dogs him for a lot of his journey.

This shadow is an interesting thing to analyse. At first, I took it to mean depression, or any kind of black emotional state that can cloud one's judgement and ability to see things clearly. As it turns out, the shadow is Doubt, and stops Anodos seeing the magic of Fairyland and all its beauty and wonder. It follows him like a curse throughout the book, and his thoughts about it and what it does to him can often be poignant.

Anodos falls in love with a woman who is literally an object, and his love is based entirely on her beauty. For a modern reader this is a tad annoying. However, for the Victorians versed in the spirit of medieval revival, the tradition of courtly love was all about the unattainable lady. Ladies were worshipped from afar, idealised to the point that their depictions bordered on otherworldly, and those that loved them raised them high on pedestals (a notion that is literalised in a section of the book where Anodos serenades his lady into existence onto the top of an actual pedestal). Beauty and grace were worshipped and lovers were inspired to better themselves, emotionally, spiritually, and physically in order to attain their lady.

Everything Anodos goes through is to help him grow, so many people take *Phantastes* to be an allegory for growing up, meaning that Fairyland is the adult world, and the protagonist, at 21 is just new to it and exploring all its beauty and all its nightmares. Although MacDonald was a minister and preacher, *Phantastes* isn't a religious allegory—in fact with Anodos' behaviour in mind, you could argue that the book advocates exercising free will and disobedience as the route to personal growth rather than faith.

To read *Phantastes* as science fiction, you have to dig deeper. Undeniably, it fits into the fantasy genre, but science seems virtually absent from it on first glance. However, prolific Scottish literature critic Cairns Craig, makes a claim for its inclusion in the SF canon, saying that the book reflects knowledge of the energy science theories of James Clerk Maxwell (another Scot, and Professor at Aberdeen University after MacDonald left) which were the most innovative theories in energy physics since Newton. Craig points to the passage in *Phantastes* where the solid physical matter of Anodos' sink and carpet dissolve into water and grass as an example of MacDonald imaginatively exploring the possibilities of Maxwell's theories of shifting, eternal energies able to transform into other things. In the fantasy genre, strange occurrences like this can be explained by magic, whereas in science fiction, the same things can be explained through science. *Phantastes*, though still rooted in the magical, dabbles in this kind of scientific thought, although the ultimate explanations are magical. The book is a strange mixture of both fantasy and science fiction in this regard.

Also, if we consider the two basic functions of modern science fiction—to imagine a future or a different world out of *what if* possibilities, and secondly, to hold up a mirror to our own world through the means of creating another—we see that science fiction and fantasy both have this in common.

Another interesting extract within *Phantastes* that has the potential to lean into science fiction, is the embedded narrative of a Czech university student who falls in love with a woman who lives inside a magic mirror. She inhabits the world inside the mirror and interacts with the objects in the room's reflection, but does not appear physically in student's room. Reading it as a fantasy story, it's a magical curse, but I have previously read SF stories where instead of a mirror it's a monitor or a screen, and instead of magic, it's a blip in spacetime, resulting in an overlap of parallel universes. MacDonald would not have had these kinds of ideas in mind in 1858, but his imagination and curiosity for fantastic and scientific possibilities would have made him a very good SF writer if he was around today. Certainly, the imagination and fascination with other worlds seems to run in his family—his grandson, Philip MacDonald, who wrote many books in the 1930s-60s under different pen-names, including W.J. Stuart—wrote 'the book of the film' for *Forbidden Planet*.

Another surprising revelation, for me at least, was this: when I was doing my research for this piece, scanning along the library shelf, I was shocked to read the title of another of George MacDonald's books—*The Princess and the Goblin*. The adventures of Curdie and Princess Irene, in the cartoon adaptation, was one of my favourite films as a child, and I'm sure I'm not alone. In childhood, of course, you never consider the authors, and I never questioned that a cartoon even had one. I never would have dreamed that it was written in the 1850s by a man from my town, and alumni of the University of Aberdeen, who, about 150 years ago, walked the same streets I do every day.

It could be said that his roots were romantically Celtic—a background Walter Scott would have loved: he was a direct descendant of the Highland clan, the MacDonalds of Glencoe. His ancestors escaped the infamous Massacre of Glencoe, and others fought alongside the Jacobites in the Battle of Culloden in 1745. George MacDonald himself was born into a respected farming family in 1824 near Huntly, north Aberdeenshire. At university, he was known to be a well-liked, handsome, intellectual and morally upright man who loved romance literature and daydreaming and kept company with poets and philosophers. He turned to religion after university, apparently a natural preacher, and became a Minister at a Congregational Church in Arundel, Sussex in England. He married and had children there, and it was around this time he began to write seriously. His first publication in 1855 was a dramatic play-poem called *Within and Without*. When his unorthodox views upset his conservative congregation in Arundel, he was forced to resign. He relocated to Manchester where he made his career preaching and lecturing. His first prose book was *Phantastes*, but he didn't become an established success until his following book, *David Elginbrod*, a story of peasant life in Aberdeenshire, a lot of it written in Aberdonian Doric. From there, he went on to become an eminent, well-known writer and preacher living in London. In addition to influencing Carroll and Lewis, he also had a huge impact on Charles Kingsley who wrote *The Water Babies*. He was also acquainted with (and apparently photographed alongside) Alfred Lord Tennyson, Charles Dickens, William Makepeace Thackery and Wilkie Collins, to name but a few. Mark Twain came to see him in England and over in America, he was friends with Walt Whitman. MacDonald enjoyed a long career and a long life, writing many works of fantasy, non-fiction and poetry, before passing away in 1905.

*Phantastes* is an enchanting book, best enjoyed while relaxing in the shade beneath a gently whispering tree. To ponder over it is like analysing a dream, but I'd recommend reading it in shorter sittings. It has so many beautiful moments, but one of my favourite things to take away from has to be this very simply-put proverb: 'Past tears are present strength'. With its high-flown Victorian style, it may not be the book everyone dives to read nowadays, but the world of fantasy and science fiction literature has a lot to thank it for.

Art: Jessica Good

# Phantastes

George MacDonald

# Chapter IV

**B**y this time, my hostess was quite anxious that I should be gone. So, with warm thanks for their hospitality, I took my leave, and went my way through the little garden towards the forest. Some of the garden flowers had wandered into the wood, and were growing here and there along the path, but the trees soon became too thick and shadowy for them. I particularly noticed some tall lilies, which grew on both sides of the way, with large dazzlingly white flowers, set off by the universal green. It was now dark enough for me to see that every flower was shining with a light of its own. Indeed it was by this light that I saw them, an internal, peculiar light, proceeding from each, and not reflected from a common source of light as in the daytime. This light sufficed only for the plant itself, and was not strong enough to cast any but the faintest shadows around it, or to illuminate any of the neighbouring objects with other than the faintest tinge of its own individual hue. From the lilies above mentioned, from the campanulas, from the foxgloves, and every bell-shaped flower, curious little figures shot up their heads, peeped at me, and drew back. They seemed to inhabit them, as snails their shells but I was sure some of them were intruders, and belonged to the gnomes or goblin-fairies, who inhabit the ground and earthy creeping plants. From the cups of Arum lilies, creatures with great heads and grotesque faces shot up like Jack-in-the-box, and made grimaces at me; or rose slowly and slily over the edge of the cup, and spouted water at me, slipping suddenly back, like those little soldier-crabs that inhabit the shells of sea-snails. Passing a row of tall thistles, I saw them crowded with little faces, which peeped every one from behind its flower, and drew back as quickly; and I heard them saying to each other, evidently intending me to hear, but the speaker always hiding behind his tuft, when I looked in his direction, "Look at him! Look at him! He has begun a story without a beginning, and it will never have any end. He! he! he! Look at him!"

But as I went further into the wood, these sights and sounds became fewer, giving way to others of a different character. A little forest of wild hyacinths was alive with exquisite creatures, who stood nearly motionless, with drooping necks, holding each by the stem of her flower, and swaying gently with it, whenever a low breath of wind swung the crowded floral belfry. In like manner, though differing of course in form and meaning, stood a group of harebells, like little angels waiting, ready, till they were wanted to go on some yet unknown message. In darker nooks, by the mossy roots of the trees, or in little tufts of grass, each dwelling in a globe of its own green light, weaving a network of grass and its shadows, glowed the glowworms.

They were just like the glowworms of our own land, for they are fairies everywhere; worms in the day, and glowworms at night, when their own can appear, and they can be themselves to others as well as themselves. But they had their enemies here. For I saw great strong-armed beetles, hurrying about with most unwieldy haste, awkward as elephant-calves, looking apparently for glowworms; for the moment a beetle espied one, through what to it was a forest of grass, or an underwood of moss, it pounced upon it, and bore it away, in spite of its feeble resistance. Wondering what their object could be, I watched one of the beetles, and then I discovered a thing I could not account for. But it is no use trying to account for things in Fairy Land; and one who travels there soon learns to forget the very idea of doing so, and takes everything as it comes; like a child, who, being in a chronic condition of wonder, is surprised at nothing. What I saw was this. Everywhere, here and there over the ground, lay little, dark-looking lumps of something more like earth than anything else, and about the size of a chestnut. The beetles hunted in couples for these; and having found one, one of them stayed to watch it, while the other hurried to find a glowworm. By signals, I presume, between them, the latter soon found his companion again: they then took the glowworm and held its luminous tail to the dark earthly pellet; when lo, it shot up into the air like a sky-rocket, seldom, however, reaching the height of the highest tree. Just like a rocket too, it burst in the air, and fell in a shower of the most gorgeously coloured sparks of every variety of hue; golden and red, and purple and green, and blue and rosy fires crossed and inter-crossed each other, beneath the shadowy heads, and between the columnar stems of the forest trees. They never used the same glowworm twice, I observed; but let him go, apparently uninjured by the use they had made of him.

In other parts, the whole of the immediately surrounding foliage was illuminated by the interwoven dances in the air of splendidly coloured fire-flies, which sped hither and thither, turned, twisted, crossed, and recrossed, entwining every complexity of intervolved motion. Here and there, whole mighty trees glowed with an emitted phosphorescent light. You could trace the very course of the great roots in the earth by the faint light that came through; and every twig, and every vein on every leaf was a streak of pale fire.

All this time, as I went through the wood, I was haunted with the feeling that other shapes, more like my own size and mien, were moving about at a little distance on all sides of me. But as yet I could discern none of them, although the moon was high enough to send a great many of her rays down between the trees, and these rays were unusually bright, and sight-giving, notwithstanding she was only a half-moon. I constantly imagined, however, that forms were visible in all directions except that to which my gaze was turned; and that they only became invisible, or resolved themselves into other woodland shapes, the moment my looks were directed towards them. However this may have been, except for this feeling of presence, the woods seemed utterly bare of anything like human companionship, although my glance often fell on some object which I fancied to be a human form; for I soon found that I was quite deceived; as, the moment I fixed my regard on it, it showed plainly that it was a bush, or a tree, or a rock.

Soon a vague sense of discomfort possessed me. With variations of relief, this gradually increased; as if some evil thing were wandering about in my neighbourhood, sometimes nearer and sometimes further off, but still approaching. The feeling continued and deepened, until all my pleasure in the shows of various kinds that everywhere betokened the presence of the merry fairies vanished by degrees, and left me full of anxiety and fear, which I was unable to associate with any definite object whatever. At length the thought crossed my mind with horror: "Can it be possible that the Ash is looking for me? Or that, in his nightly wanderings, his path is gradually verging towards mine?" I comforted myself, however, by remembering that he had started quite in another direction; one that would lead him, if he kept it, far apart from me; especially as, for the last two or three hours, I had been diligently journeying eastward. I kept on my way, therefore, striving by direct effort of the will against the encroaching fear; and to this end occupying my mind, as much as I could, with other thoughts. I was so far successful that, although I was conscious, if I yielded for a moment, I should be almost overwhelmed with horror, I was yet able to walk right on for an hour or more. What I feared I could not tell. Indeed, I was left in a state of the vaguest uncertainty as regarded the nature of my enemy, and knew not the mode or object of his attacks; for, somehow or other, none of my questions had succeeded in drawing a definite answer from the dame in the cottage. How then to defend myself I knew not; nor even by what sign I might with certainty recognise the presence of my foe; for as yet this vague though powerful fear was all the indication of danger I had. To add to my distress, the clouds in the west had risen nearly to the top of the skies, and they and the moon were travelling slowly towards each other. Indeed, some of their advanced guard had already met her, and she had begun to wade through a filmy vapour that gradually deepened.

At length she was for a moment almost entirely obscured. When she shone out again, with a brilliancy increased by the contrast, I saw plainly on the path before me—from around which at this spot the trees receded, leaving a small space of green sward—the shadow of a large hand, with knotty joints and protuberances here and there. Especially I remarked, even in the midst of my fear, the bulbous points of the fingers. I looked hurriedly all around, but could see nothing from which such a shadow should fall. Now, however, that I had a direction, however undetermined, in which to project my apprehension, the very sense of danger and need of action overcame that stifling which is the worst property of fear. I reflected in a moment, that if this were indeed a shadow, it was useless to look for the object that cast it in any other direction than between the shadow and the moon. I looked, and peered, and intensified my vision, all to no purpose. I could see nothing of that kind, not even an ash-tree in the neighbourhood. Still the shadow remained; not steady, but moving to and fro, and once I saw the fingers close, and grind themselves close, like the claws of a wild animal, as if in uncontrollable longing for some anticipated prey.

There seemed but one mode left of discovering the substance of this shadow. I went forward boldly, though with an inward shudder which I would not heed, to the spot where the shadow lay, threw myself on the ground, laid my head within the form of the hand, and turned my eyes towards the moon Good heavens! what did I see? I wonder that ever I arose, and that the very shadow of the hand did not hold me where I lay until fear had frozen my brain. I saw the strangest figure; vague, shadowy, almost transparent, in the central parts, and gradually deepening in substance towards the outside, until it ended in extremities capable of casting such a shadow as fell from the hand, through the awful fingers of which I now saw the moon. The hand was uplifted in the attitude of a paw about to strike its prey. But the face, which throbbed with fluctuating and pulsatory visibility—not from changes in the light it reflected, but from changes in its own conditions of reflecting power, the alterations being from within, not from without—it was horrible. I do not know how to describe it. It caused a new sensation. Just as one cannot translate a horrible odour, or a ghastly pain, or a fearful sound, into words, so I cannot describe this new form of awful hideousness. I can only try to describe something that is not it, but seems somewhat parallel to it; or at least is suggested by it. It reminded me of what I had heard of vampires; for the face resembled that of a corpse more than anything else I can think of; especially when I can conceive such a face in motion, but not suggesting any life as the source of the motion. The features were rather handsome than otherwise, except the mouth, which had scarcely a curve in it. The lips were of equal thickness; but the thickness was not at all remarkable, even although they looked slightly swollen. They seemed fixedly open, but were not wide apart. Of course I did not *remark* these lineaments at the time: I was too horrified for that. I noted them afterwards, when the form returned on my inward sight with a vividness too intense to admit of my doubting the accuracy of the reflex. But the most awful of the features were the eyes. These were alive, yet not with life.

They seemed lighted up with an infinite greed. A gnawing voracity, which devoured the devourer, seemed to be the indwelling and propelling power of the whole ghostly apparition. I lay for a few moments simply imbruted with terror; when another cloud, obscuring the moon, delivered me from the immediately paralysing effects of the presence to the vision of the object of horror, while it added the force of imagination to the power of fear within me; inasmuch as, knowing far worse cause for apprehension than before, I remained equally ignorant from what I had to defend myself, or how to take any precautions: he might be upon me in the darkness any moment. I sprang to my feet, and sped I knew not whither, only away from the spectre. I thought no longer of the path, and often narrowly escaped dashing myself against a tree, in my headlong flight of fear.

Great drops of rain began to patter on the leaves. Thunder began to mutter, then growl in the distance. I ran on. The rain fell heavier. At length the thick leaves could hold it up no longer; and, like a second firmament, they poured their torrents on the earth. I was soon drenched, but that was nothing. I came to a small swollen stream that rushed through the woods. I had a vague hope that if I crossed this stream, I should be in safety from my pursuer; but I soon found that my hope was as false as it was vague. I dashed across the stream, ascended a rising ground, and reached a more open space, where stood only great trees. Through them I directed my way, holding eastward as nearly as I could guess, but not at all certain that I was not moving in an opposite direction. My mind was just reviving a little from its extreme terror, when, suddenly, a flash of lightning, or rather a cataract of successive flashes, behind me, seemed to throw on the ground in front of me, but far more faintly than before, from the extent of the source of the light, the shadow of the same horrible hand. I sprang forward, stung to yet wilder speed; but had not run many steps before my foot slipped, and, vainly attempting to recover myself, I fell at the foot of one of the large trees. Half-stunned, I yet raised myself, and almost involuntarily looked back. All I saw was the hand within three feet of my face. But, at the same moment, I felt two large soft arms thrown round me from behind; and a voice like a woman's said: "Do not fear the goblin; he dares not hurt you now." With that, the hand was suddenly withdrawn as from a fire, and disappeared in the darkness and the rain. Overcome with the mingling of terror and joy, I lay for some time almost insensible. The first thing I remember is the sound of a voice above me, full and low, and strangely reminding me of the sound of a gentle wind amidst the leaves of a great tree. It murmured over and over again: "I may love him, I may love him; for he is a man, and I am only a beech-tree." I found I was seated on the ground, leaning against a human form, and supported still by the arms around me, which I knew to be those of a woman who must be rather above the human size, and largely proportioned. I turned my head, but without moving otherwise, for I feared lest the arms should untwine themselves; and clear, somewhat mournful eyes met mine. At least that is how they impressed me; but I could see very little of colour or outline as we sat in the dark and rainy shadow of the tree. The face seemed very lovely, and solemn from its stillness; with the aspect of one who is quite content, but waiting for something. I saw my conjecture from her arms was correct: she was above the human scale throughout, but not greatly.

"Why do you call yourself a beech-tree?" I said.

"Because I am one," she replied, in the same low, musical, murmuring voice.

"You are a woman," I returned.

"Do you think so? Am I very like a woman then?"

"You are a very beautiful woman. Is it possible you should not know it?"

"I am very glad you think so. I fancy I feel like a woman sometimes. I do so to-night—and always when the rain drips from my hair. For there is an old prophecy in our woods that one day we shall all be men and women like you. Do you know anything about it in your region? Shall I be very happy when I am a woman? I fear not, for it is always in nights like these that I feel like one. But I long to be a woman for all that."

I had let her talk on, for her voice was like a solution of all musical sounds. I now told her that I could hardly say whether women were happy or not. I knew one who had not been happy; and for my part, I had often longed for Fairy Land, as she now longed for the world of men. But then neither of us had lived long, and perhaps people grew happier as they grew older. Only I doubted it.

I could not help sighing. She felt the sigh, for her arms were still round me. She asked me how old I was.

"Twenty-one," said I.

"Why, you baby!" said she, and kissed me with the sweetest kiss of winds and odours. There was a cool faithfulness in the kiss that revived my heart wonderfully. I felt that I feared the dreadful Ash no more.

"What did the horrible Ash want with me?" I said.

"I am not quite sure, but I think he wants to bury you at the foot of his tree. But he shall not touch you, my child."

"Are all the ash-trees as dreadful as he?"

"Oh, no. They are all disagreeable selfish creatures—(what horrid men they will make, if it be true!)—but this one has a hole in his heart that nobody knows of but one or two; and he is always trying to fill it up, but he cannot. That must be what he wanted you for. I wonder if he will ever be a man. If he is, I hope they will kill him."

"How kind of you to save me from him!"

"I will take care that he shall not come near you again. But there are some in the wood more like me, from whom, alas! I cannot protect you. Only if you see any of them very beautiful, try to walk round them."

"What then?"

"I cannot tell you more. But now I must tie some of my hair about you, and then the Ash will not touch you. Here, cut some off. You men have strange cutting things about you."

She shook her long hair loose over me, never moving her arms.

"I cannot cut your beautiful hair. It would be a shame."

"Not cut my hair! It will have grown long enough before any is wanted again in this wild forest. Perhaps it may never be of any use again—not till I am a woman." And she sighed.

As gently as I could, I cut with a knife a long tress of flowing, dark hair, she hanging her beautiful head over me. When I had finished, she shuddered and breathed deep, as one does when an acute pain, steadfastly endured without sign of suffering, is at length relaxed. She then took the hair and tied it round me, singing a strange, sweet song, which I could not understand, but which left in me a feeling like this—

I saw thee ne'er before;
I see thee never more;
But love, and help, and pain, beautiful one,
Have made thee mine, till all my years are done.

I cannot put more of it into words. She closed her arms about me again, and went on singing. The rain in the leaves, and a light wind that had arisen, kept her song company. I was wrapt in a trance of still delight. It told me the secret of the woods, and the flowers, and the birds. At one time I felt as if I was wandering in childhood through sunny spring forests, over carpets of primroses, anemones, and little white starry things—I had almost said creatures, and finding new wonderful flowers at every turn. At another, I lay half dreaming in the hot summer noon, with a book of old tales beside me, beneath a great beech; or, in autumn, grew sad because I trod on the leaves that had sheltered me, and received their last blessing in the sweet odours of decay; or, in a winter evening, frozen still, looked up, as I went home to a warm fireside, through the netted boughs and twigs to the cold, snowy moon, with her opal zone around her. At last I had fallen asleep; for I know nothing more that passed till I found myself lying under a superb beech-tree, in the clear light of the morning, just before sunrise. Around me was a girdle of fresh beech-leaves. Alas! I brought nothing with me out of Fairy Land, but memories— memories. The great boughs of the beech hung drooping around me. At my head rose its smooth stem, with its great sweeps of curving surface that swelled like undeveloped limbs. The leaves and branches above kept on the song which had sung me asleep; only now, to my mind, it sounded like a farewell and a speedwell. I sat a long time, unwilling to go; but my unfinished story urged me on. I must act and wander. With the sun well risen, I rose, and put my arms as far as they would reach around the beech-tree, and kissed it, and said good-bye. A trembling went through the leaves; a few of the last drops of the night's rain fell from off them at my feet; and as I walked slowly away, I seemed to hear in a whisper once more the words: "I may love him, I may love him; for he is a man, and I am only a beech-tree."

# Interview: Simon Morden

Simon Morden's *Metrozone* (Petrovich) Trilogy, *Equations of Life, Theories of Flight* & *Degrees of Freedom* won the Philip K. Dick Award. The adventures continued with The *Curve of the Earth*. Currently the author is writing a series of novels about Down, a world linked to London by a network of mysterious portals. *Down Station* was released at the beginning of the year, with *The White City* out in October. Here Simon Morden talks to Gary Dalkin.

**Gary Dalkin**: *Down Station* was published in February, and when I reviewed it for Vector I wrote that it felt rather like a Young Adult novel, and wondered if it might not have been better marketed that way. It also seemed very much like a set-up novel, introducing the world of Down and a group of characters—most prominently the dutiful 19-year-old Sikh engineering student Dalip and 18-year-old Mary, streetwise from being in and out of care all her life—then giving them an initial adventure and setting them on a quest to reach the possibly mythical White City. It seemed there could be an indefinite number of adventures along the way before anyone ever reached the city, but then the title of the second book in the series was announced as *The White City*, so it's not giving anything away to say that some of the characters from *Down Station* do, eventually, reach their destination. At which point I think it's worth noting that *The White City* feels like a very different book to its predecessor: Mary and Dalip have really matured from when we first met them: no one turns into a dragon and there are no magical battles. Rather, we get pirates, some pointers towards a much bigger picture, and find the White City is not at all what we might have expected. With all that said, how important is it to you that each book has its own distinctive feel? Surprising developments towards the end of *The White City* leave possibilities for the series wide open. It feels now like the story could go in all sorts of directions, and that's rather exciting …

**Simon Morden**: I could, if I wanted to, write the same story over and over again with the serial numbers filed off. It makes sense to give readers a predictable, satisfying read that isn't too challenging, and to repeat that formula and build a brand. Publishers love that. Marketing really loves that. And it works. It works incredibly well across all genres—from crime and thrillers, through war stories and family sagas, historical novels and fantasy, to science fiction. People make careers out of writing variations of the same book for their entire lives. Kudos to them: they've found their audience and they know how to please them. We are, for all our artistic pretensions, part of the entertainment industry: an industry which is worth £70bn to the UK economy. We shouldn't lose sight of that.

Having laid all that on the table, I have to acknowledge that I don't do that. I could do that, but I don't. Writing books is a solitary task. It involves locking yourself away for hundreds of hours and fashioning a vicarious experience out of nothing but the same twenty-six letters and some random pieces of punctuation. If I'm going to subject myself to that discipline, then I'm going to want to, at the very least, entertain myself. So, in the initial draft stage, I'm writing for an audience of precisely one: me. I appreciate that might make me sound like a terrible narcissist, but, really? If I'm not enjoying it, I strongly suspect that anyone who subsequently reads the story isn't going to either.

I've tried to make every book I've written different from the previous one. For the *Petrovitch* books, *Equations of Life* is a flat-out, old school cyberpunk thriller. *Theories of Flight* is my war story. *Degrees of Freedom* a Cold War spy caper. *The Curve of the Earth* is a bastard mutation of a buddy film. The fifth book (written, unpublished) is different again. And so on: *Arcanum* is an epic fantasy that turns by degrees into the most science fiction story I've ever written.

On to Down. It was interesting to hear your thoughts on whether it should have been marketed as YA—there is, of course, nothing to stop the teenagers finding it for themselves. My moral compass regarding what can and can't go in a YA novel is somewhat skewed in that I grew up reading adult SFF, with all the sex, violence and drugs that involved. So maybe Lovecraftian existential horror and pit-fighting wild animals are good to go. I'll mention it to my editor!

This is a really long answer to a relatively simple question, for which I apologise. Yes, *The White City* is a different type of story to *Down Station*. It's a continuation but, inevitably and naturally, it's going to be different story, because the protagonists are growing in their understanding of how Down works and are becoming more comfortable in their new roles. So, Pirates! Adventure! Treasure! And all the weirdness of *The White City* we can't talk about.

The end? I loved writing that. I didn't know it was going to happen until it happened. Dalip's surprise is my own. The possibilities are now, literally, limitless.


**GD**: Which leads me to something I've been wondering about. Given you didn't know what was going to happen until it happened, how much do you plan and plot in advance, either with these books or in general? I'd assumed that you knew essentially all about Down, this strange world where people from various times find themselves when fleeing from London for various reasons, but clearly it can surprise you as much as the reader. And sort of allied to that question, which came first: the world in which the Down novels are set, or the central characters? And if the world came first, how do you decide whose story to tell within that setting? Presumably, given the right circumstances, anyone in London could find themselves in Down …


**SM**: This is where I get to sound like the Worst Author Ever. Either that or the Wizard of Oz, dazzling you with magic when it's all done with mirrors. I don't plan. I don't plan at all. Sometimes I have an end point but no beginning. Sometimes

I have a beginning but no idea where it's going to go. Sometimes I have several ideas that I'm kicking around and they'll suddenly line up in my conscious mind as being related. My preferred method of writing is simply to sit down and write, describing the scene to myself as I go along, then stitching another on after that, and so on until I'm done. I don't know when I start how long it's going to be, or anything about the plot arc. I'm literally making it up. When I reach the end, whenever that is, I stop.

That, of course, means that it can get problematic when I work with big publishers who want to see an outline, not just of book one, but of any subsequent books in a series. We've pretty much come to an arrangement now where I write something that sounds feasible, and they don't hold me to it when I give them the manuscript. I do, of course, then have to turn in something that's just as good as the outline, if not better.

It also means that I end up writing a fair bit more than gets published, because I'm off on a frolic of my own, outside of any contract, just putting the words down and indulging my flights of fancy. If the result is good, then I'll write a proposal based on what I've actually written, and I'm able to hand any interested party a fully-functioning draft if they're interested. I acknowledge that it's a ridiculous way to work. Sometimes, it doesn't matter: *Equations of Life* was written before I sold it. *Down Station* was written before I sold it. *The White City* outline possibly vaguely resembles the *The White City* that's being published in October. Sometimes, I can end up spending a year on a project that goes nowhere. But please, don't try this at home. You'd have to be mad to do it the way I do.

So I should really answer the question now, shouldn't I? *Down* wasn't planned. I didn't work out the magic system before I started. The only clues I had were was the idea of opening the door and seeing a whole new world, and a series of Channel 4 documentaries I remembered about night workers on the London Underground. I wrote about the people I saw in those programmes, to start off with. There are no natives to Down— so people like Crows and Bell are also part of that 'anyone in the right circumstances' scenario. Everyone you eventually meet has a story of coming to Down. I just started with my protagonists, and described their experiences of Down as they happened. I have to trust my subconscious a lot, that it will have already done the heavy lifting by the time I need to set something in stone. Mostly it works. Sometimes, it needs a bit more editing than otherwise would be necessary.

That's how I do it. I suppose I didn't know any better, and now I'm entrenched in that way of working, and can't stop.

**GD**: Mary and Dalip work well as a contrasting pair of protagonists. A more conventional writer would likely have put them together romantically by now, but there's no sign of that, which is refreshing. Dalip is an interesting choice of character, in that Sikhs feature rarely in SF and Fantasy, a notable exception being perhaps Walter Jon Williams' *Days of Atonement*. Was Dalip inspired by one of the people featured in the Channel 4 documentaries? He takes his faith very seriously, and while the books don't touch much on the spiritual side of his beliefs, he has a very strong moral sensibility. How was it, yourself being a Christian, writing about a member of a different faith, especially in terms of understanding how Dalip sees the world and getting him 'right'? More generally, how much does your Christian faith inform your fiction? Was there a particular concern to ensure that Dalip was a fully rounded character, which he clearly is, and not a stock representative of his religion? Was there even some worry from your publishers that your portrayal might cause offense—I'm remembering when JK Rowling was attacked by Sikh leaders in India for her portrayal of a Sikh character in *The Casual Vacancy*.

**SM**: Regarding Mary and Dalip's friendship. Yes, I'm aware that in any given stressful situation, standard operating procedure is that two people of compatible sexualities will inevitably become romantically attached, the strength and speed of such bonding being directly proportional to the degree of threat. If one saves the other's life, then it's an absolute and inviolable law of the universe that they'll fall in love … because that's what happens in real life.

Referring back to my answer in a previous question, I didn't know whether they were going to become a couple. They're of similar age, but that's about the only thing they have in common. Their life experiences are radically different, and if it wasn't for Down, they'd never have met. It was much more likely that they'd spend their time trying to get on, because that's what circumstances demanded, while not really getting on, because each one thought the other was a bit of an idiot. That's what you see to start off with. It's only as they get to understand each other do they relax into each other's company, and even then more things happen to make their trajectories diverge rather than converge.

And yes, I wanted a similar diverse cast of characters that I saw on the documentary—all I did was bring it up to date to reflect the recent demographic changes in London, even if that did leave me open to criticism from the *Daily Mail* for being 'dutifully multicultural'. I'm not quite sure which London the reviewer thought I was writing about, but I've been subsequently assured that my fiction is more realistic than her reality.

So Dalip wasn't a deliberate choice, in the sense that none of my choices are particularly deliberate. That he's a young Sikh man, brought up in the faith, beginning to work out what it means for him, rather than simply following his parents' expectations of Sikhism, is part of who he is, and not an overlay to make him more interesting, or provide narrative drive. I agree it's not that common, but there was no good reason to exclude him. So I didn't.

On to the whole 'what do I write' question, and cultural appropriation and the entirely inescapable fact that I'm a mostly-white, British, English-as-first-language, fifty-year-old heterosexual male, writing

about things that are outside my immediate experience. I'd argue that part of the writers' skill, and probably the most critical part for a writer of fiction to possess, is the ability provide vicarious experiences. Using words to describe a place you've never been to, to describe a scene you've never witnessed, to describe a character you've never met: it's something that all fiction writers have to do in order to construct the story they're telling. You have to bring these things to life, not metaphorically but literally. You have to breathe life into them.

If you don't put the time and trouble into fashioning your creations as perfectly as you can, then when you try to bring them to life, it can go horribly wrong. Have I just made a Frankenstein analogy? I'm going to fall back on Tolkien now, who viewed his imagining of Middle Earth as an act of sub-creation: not sub as in substandard, but sub as in secondary. As a Catholic, he viewed his creative urge as part of what it meant to be made in God's image. I want to make that theological and philosophical insight part of the scaffolding that supports my writing.

And with that underpinning the way I tell stories, I don't think there should be any no-go areas for writers. None. We—whatever culture we come from, whatever our skin colour, our ethnic heritage, our class, our gender—have to have the freedom to write about whatever we feel drawn to. That doesn't mean we can't be held accountable for what we write: Rowling's perfectly free to include a Sikh family in a book, and Sikh leaders are free to tell her she made a hash of it—with an acknowledgement that UK Sikhs then criticised the critics for trying to sweep the problems Rowling was highlighting under the carpet. The idea of a monolithic cultural identity is long past its sell-by date: we wouldn't dream of doing it for ourselves, so why impose it on others?

Which is all a very long way around of saying that the only person Dalip represents is Dalip. Another Sikh would react differently in the same situation—much mention is made of Dalip's grandfather, a World War Two veteran of the Far East campaign. Swap those two over, and you'd have a very different book indeed, and I try my absolute hardest not to write characters that are interchangeable. Whether I succeed is an exercise left to the reader. Gollancz expressed no misgivings whatsoever. They are, of course, brilliantly on-the-ball, and I'd have been told during the editing process if they thought I'd done something badly.

I do want to talk briefly about *Arcanum*, which involved exactly no white British people at all. It was set in Alpine Carinthia, and the entire cast was either Jewish, pagan Europeans, or dwarves. Expressions of medieval Judaism and Germanic paganism in a fantasy setting was part of the characters' lives: why wouldn't I write about them, involve them in the plot, have people discuss differences in practice and theology? If you're a good writer, that's what you do. You don't ignore the religious beliefs of your characters.

Finally, if one of the questions you're asking is, 'Do you feel compelled to wedge evangelical Christianity into everything you write?', the answer is emphatically no. Otherwise, it's very difficult for me to say how my own faith affects my writing, because it's an intrinsic part of me: I'd argue that it's impossible for me to untangle everything. I'm sure there are themes I keep coming back to, character types I deal with in different ways, but again, that's probably better discussed by people who aren't me. How it affects me as a writer is more straight-forward: behave professionally, honour contracts and confidences, meet deadlines and fans, treat everyone with respect, listen to your editor, and don't be a dick. Those attributes aren't exclusive to Christianity, or any particular religion, but it keeps me on the straight and narrow.

**GD**: As well as *The White City*, you wrote a story which I commissioned for the anthology *Improbable Botany*, which all being well should be coming out towards the end of the year. I think 'Shine' is a really powerful story, with a striking ending. Did you find any particular challenges in crafting botanical SF? Are writers missing a trick not exploring botany more in fiction?

**SM**: I'm what you'd call a 'hard' scientist: a first degree in geology and a PhD in planetary geophysics, so there's been a lot of inorganic chemistry and physics along the way. The only biology has really been taxonomy of fossils—and plants don't have too many hard parts to preserve. It's been a slow realisation—not just through gardening, but generally paying attention—that plant life dominates the biosphere to an incredible degree. If we find basic life somewhere, it's going to be an algae analogue.

Writing an SF story where plants were a significant factor in the plot has been part of a natural progression, but it's one which, yes, a lot of writers ignore, and I did it myself. But there's no excuse: *The Martian*, with its potato-based heroics, John Wyndham's *Triffids* (and *Lichen*), Christopher's *Death of Grass*, and Wells' red weed (from *The War of the Worlds*) are all examples of SF botany done well. Any terraforming attempt will have atmosphere modification by plants as virtually top priority. Plants supply building materials, medicines, food, clothing, air ... yes. More plants.

**GD**: Finally, what's next? Presumably at least one more Down novel, but do you have any other works in progress that we'll be reading in the next two or three years? Or is it too early to say yet where your imagination might take you?

**SM**: I've finished works aplenty looking for homes—Petrovitch 5 is waiting for contractual wranglings to be settled—and other novel-length works doing the usual rounds. After Down 3, I've several other things I'd like to write, but some of that's dependent on what publishers want. I'm also doing on spec work—I've just sold a novella to Ian Whaite's NewCon Press I'm very happy with, as it's proper old school deep space SF, and I'm half-way through what will probably be a novel-length standalone work, about a little robot probe exploring a huge new planet: ours.

# Noise and Sparks 2: You Have to Live

## Ruth EJ Booth

**"You have to live," he'd said.**

I recall this in the refuge of my study; but, out of the door behind me, waits chaos. Paper and stationery, plates and glass knick-knacks, laundry, books, electrical whoozits and whatsits, all gathered into higgledy heaps and ill-fitted boxstacks; as if freeze-framed in some strangely organized game of Katamari Damacy. I'm moving, and it could be the biggest mistake of my life.

The decision itself was startlingly easy, but recently, it's gained a foreboding weight. This doesn't feel right. It seems selfish to leave a life that's supported me for half a decade for something that might make me happier, but is, unquestionably, much less secure. Even if this works out, it'll mean less time for my writing—my passion; my cherished bolt-hole when the world gets too, too much. Half the reason I'm writing this column right now is so I don't have to think about all the clearing and packing still left to do.

So much rests on what's to come. Yet I've no compass for what I'm about to do; no plan should it all fall apart. Frankly, I'm terrified. It's not a decision I'd have made six years ago. But then, writing SF wasn't part of the plan either.

Fiction found me when I most needed it, bubbling up under the surface of a bunch of shitty, directionless years, and a chance taken on a local writing class. Its discovery was a revelation, a relief I could feel this exhilarated about something again; regret, for years spent without. So this was how it felt to be truly passionate about something … I threw myself into it, heart and soul. Those moments when you barely feel the keyboard or the pen on paper for what's flowing through your fingertips, I lived for them like I'd nothing else. When people talk about what makes a writer, that feeling of flow is the closest I've found to an answer. And if there's any great secret to writing, it can only be this—to find that feeling, and chase it for the rest of your days.

But what do you do when that isn't enough anymore?

The realization can be a horrifically lonely one. Oftentimes, you only admit the truth to yourself when it starts affecting your writing, pushing at the edge of thought, intruder in your idyll. This hurts. You have reading, and you have movies, and games, but as a break turns into something longer, when it's clear it's not just a case of painting the house for a few weeks, the loss of flow—at best, the sense that writing is tainted—is hard to accept.

If admitting it to yourself is difficult, telling others is much harder, especially other writers. Creative people can be amongst the most supportive, welcoming souls you will ever meet. If you're lucky, you'll count some amongst your most treasured friends. To admit that what binds you together doesn't make you happy anymore can feel tantamount to losing your tribe.

Worst of all is the sense of inadequacy you're left with. Because … this should be enough, shouldn't it? The defining feature of an artist is love for their art. And despite the difficulties of creative life, that love should anchor them against any storm. To keep creating in trying circumstances is ennobling—romantic even. A sign of dedication to your art. Right?

So you pretend everything is fine. Hide behind the door, while your problems pile up outside. Bury yourself in so-called dedication to the work. Drive yourself on, even as that dedication becomes a sacrifice, your health and well-being for your fears. It's a dangerous, and ultimately self-destructive mindset—one that can be astonishingly difficult to get out of.

※

In her recent column on supporting a creative career[1], Zen Cho suggests any job you do alongside writing should not only keep you fed, but also stimulated, in terms of your mind and your social life. This makes sense—you can't write about people if you never spend time with them. Nor can you write if you're too tired, or too bored to think. Cho admits it's tricky to find all this in one job, but urges "if you're serious about writing, it's worth thinking about how you can arrange your life to support [that]."

But note these aren't just things you need to write. They're things you need to be fulfilled as a human being. And I don't think that's a coincidence.

Stories mean different things to different people, but at their core, they're about exploring what it means to be human—how we interact with each other, with ourselves, and the world around us. If we never allow ourselves to be human, how can we write stories that truly resonate with people at this fundamental level?

You have to live.

By the time you read this, I'll have started a Masters degree in Glasgow. It is, by all accounts, a supremely idiotic move on my part. I'm in my thirties. I don't have much money. I'm starting a career dependent on international funding and cross-border research just as our government is dissolving its strongest overseas partnership. There's probably not been a worse time to start an academic career since the advent of World War II.

And I can't remember the last time I felt this happy about where my life is going.

The odd thing is, I have writing to thank for this decision. Not just for being a bellwether for the issues in my life. If fiction hadn't come along, perhaps I never would've realized I could be happier. The loss that followed now seems like the next step in my relationship with the craft. If discovering your passion for writing is like the first flush of love, then this is the subsequent realization: that love isn't the answer to your problems, just the start of a bunch of new and much more interesting ones.

It'll be a challenge. I don't expect the guilt to just vanish. But when I think about the reasons why I'm doing this—to exercise my brain, be with good people, and work in a vibrant, creative community—I'll remember why making this decision was so easy. I won't lose writing—it'll just be another part of a well-rounded life.

Daniel José Older, in his seminal essay about the myth of writing every day[2], states that shame is the biggest enemy of creativity. "Beginning with forgiveness," he says, "revolutionizes the writing process, returns it being to a journey of creativity rather than an exercise in self-flagellation. I forgive myself for not sitting down to write sooner … for living my life … My body unclenches; a new lightness takes over once that burden has floated off. There is room, now, for story, idea, life."

So, for now, I'll start by forgiving myself. I'll allow myself the need to be more than just a writer. After all, I have to live.

---

1. Zen Cho – '5 Things for Writers to Look for in a Day Job.' http://www.writersdigest.com/editor-blogs/guide-to-literary-agents/5-things-for-writers-to-look-for-in-a-day-job shortened address: http://tinyurl.com/soi5c

2. Daniel José Older 'Writing Begins with Forgiveness: Why One of the Most Common Pieces of Writing Advice is Wrong.' http://sevenscribes.com/writing-begins-with-forgiveness-why-one-of-the-most-common-pieces-of-writing-advice-is-wrong/ shortened address: http://tinyurl.com/soi5b

---

**Ruth EJ Booth** is a writer living in Glasgow. In 2015, she won the BSFA Award for Short Fiction. For more of her non-fiction, stories and poetry, head to www.ruthbooth.com

# Reviews

**The 1000 Year Reich**
**Ian Watson**
**NEWCON Press, 248 pages**
**Review: Ian Hunter**

By my reckoning, Ian Watson has published over 30 novels since his first, *The Embedding* appeared way back in 1973. Now he has a baker's dozen of short story collections. *The 1000 Year Reich* containing 18 stories (although one of them is co-written by Watson and Roberto Quaglia) and starts with an introduction by Justina Robson. She recounts being a judge for the Arthur C. Clarke award back in 2005 when she began reading Watson's novel *Mockymen* and had to put it down and ask herself, "what is this?"

Actually, it was a novel about Nazi occult practises, nude photography and alien invasion, though even that description probably doesn't do the novel justice. Likewise, *The 1000 Year Reich* is a cornucopia of delights ranging from stories about space marines (Watson has some "previous" with Warhammer and their own space marine titles back in the day) to weird science to alternative realities and even a story that was originally published in *The Mammoth Book of Erotic Romance and Domination*. Fifteen of the stories have appeared elsewhere in the last five years, but there are three new 2016 stories original to this collection including "In Golden Armour" and "The Wild Pig's Collar."

The collection kicks off with the eponymous "The 1000 Year Reich", the inspiration for a "war is hell and chaotic especially in space" type cover illustration by Juan Miguel Aguilera. Control of space is decided by computer games, but the ultimate weapon which harnesses sexual energy is waiting to be unleashed in a tale that is totally over the top, but a hoot. In "Blair's War", a tale inspired by Watson's knowledge of Spanish history and the writings of George Orwell, Tony Blair decides Britain should intervene in the Spanish Civil War and change the course of alternative world history. If only, perhaps, when you look at what happened to Spain in the decades that followed.

Sometimes in this collection, Watson has fun with a famous book, or another genre, and in "The Name of the Lavender" we have Umberto Eco meeting Dan Brown in a head-on collision involving spies and gardeners and strange plants in a story that appeared in a very limited edition chapbook from PS Publishing which accompanied a special "best of" collection they brought out a few years ago. Watson reckons few people will have read it because copies of the chapbook are so rare that book collectors have sealed their copies away in non-biodegradable bags filled with inert gas. Lucky us, that it makes an appearance here. Likewise, we are in Dan Brown territory again in "The Arch de Triumph Code" but this time he is cunningly disguised as Don Broon from Dundee (crivens!) and about to encounter another American in Paris. Other tales involve robots, theories about how the galaxy was formed, alternative realities, solving crime, alien visitors, returning from Mars, and "Faith Without Teeth".

Is it unfair to call Ian Watson an

"old school" science fiction writer? Some of his stories could be called non-PC. Science fiction aside, I am reminded of his story "The Eye of the Ayatollah" where a religious fanatic who snatched out Ayatollah Khomeini's eye at his funeral uses it to discover where Salman Rushdie is hiding from Khomeini's fatwa. It originally appeared in *Interzone* and the very first of Steve Jones's *Best New Horror* series, and was reprinted in the 25th anniversary "best of" edition, where Jones pointed out that very few people would dare to write a story like that today, let alone publish it.

Each of the stories ends with a little postscript as Watson recounts the origin of the story or debunks some modern myths. Of particularly interest is his damning of flying saucers and UFOs, but very entertaining it is too and so are the others, even down to a description of some of Paris's less salubrious areas. Each postscript is accompanied by a picture of

Watson's head with him wearing a hat. The picture is slightly compressed, warped, distorted. It's like looking into a glass bottle and seeing the imp or genie peering back at you, waiting to get out and cause some havoc. But too late, he's here already. Recommended.

**Invisible Planets: Collected Fiction**
**Hannu Rajaniemi**
**Gollancz, 248 pages**
**Review: Iain Maloney**

Short story collections tend to fall into one of two categories. Either the author has written every story with a collection in mind, stories focused around a theme, a world or a group of characters. Alternatively the collection is made up of disparate and diverse stories already published in journals and online over years, perhaps even decades.

The former are usually more satisfying to read, the grain of ideas flowing in one direction, tone and style complimentary. As all the stories are written over a shorter period of time, the quality of the writing will be more balanced, representing a snapshot of the author's talent and interests at that time.

The latter approach can lead to uneven collections. Placing the author's first forays into the form alongside more considered stories from later in their career can offer fascinating insights into how a talent has developed, but it also tends to amplify deficiencies in weaker work. Over the course of a career style shifts, voice changes, concerns and approaches morph into new avenues of exploration until a story from the author's youth and one from middle-age can appear to be by two different writers. These books are often closer to scrap books for posterity, the work between the covers united by little more than a spine and some glue.

At first glance Hannu Rajaniemi's first collection, *Invisible Planets*, bears all the hallmarks of the latter kind of collection. After a trilogy of novels comes the short story book, perhaps at the publishers insistence, keen to keep him in the public eye in lieu of a new novel, perhaps at the writer's urging, keen to clear the decks and buy himself some time to prepare for the next novel or series. It includes his first published story, "Shibuya no Love" from 2003 and finishes with a sample of Twitter fiction. The signs were not good.

Fortunately, Rajaniemi is better than that. On the whole this is an excellent collection which captivates from the start. Rajaniemi has the kind of imagination capable of rushing off in twenty different directions—from haunted space suits through apocalyptic space battles to cities that fall in love and stalk people—while remaining firmly rooted in the one thing that makes any flight of fancy worth reading—the emotional realism at the heart of it. These stories all centre around personal relationships and regardless of whether the vehicle of exploration is an ancient horrific cult ("The Viper Blanket") or a revenge plot executed by a cat and dog team ("His Master's Voice") it is love, loss and loneliness that unites this collection.

"The Jugaad Cathedral" is a particularly good example of

'Rajaniemi is without doubt on the cutting edge'
INTERZONE

Hannu Rajaniemi

INVISIBLE PLANETS:
COLLECTED FICTION

AWARD-WINNING AUTHOR OF *THE QUANTUM THIEF*

stories, many stories are set in Rajaniemi's native Finland or in his adopted home of Edinburgh and recurring Finnish words like *perkele* (Devil) and *Saatana* (Satan) create an atmosphere of cohesion beyond the limits of theme and voice.

Two stories however let the side down. The running order is based on theme and style, like a good mixtape or playlist, rather than chronological, and reaches a natural and dramatic conclusion with the longest piece in the book, "Skywalker of Earth". The book should end there and the reader would close the cover with satisfaction, but instead we are given "Neurofiction: Introduction to "Snow White is Dead" followed by "Snow White is Dead" and "Introduction to Unused Tomorrows and Other Stories" followed by "Unused Tomorrows and Other Stories".

"Snow White..." was an experiment that Rajaniemi took part in, combining a Choose Your Own Adventure with brain-computer interfaces. The story is an approximation of what participants would have experienced. I can understand the author's urge to share what must have been a fascinating process but the story, averaged out and cut from context, is flat and disjointed while the introduction itself (and if you need a few paragraphs of non-fiction to set up a piece of fiction, you're already in a weak position) acknowledges that this is not how the story should be read or presented.

"Unused Tomorrows" is the aforementioned list of Twitter stories. While I love the idea of 140

this, exploring the widening gap between our online and offline personas through a near-future Edinburgh where social media and technology filters and controls every interaction. While Raija 'stays away from dirty networks owned by capitalists' and 'digs old computers out of dumpsters and carries then around in big shoulder bags', Kev ends their friendship in the Dwarfcraft community to 'take real life a bit more seriously', misunderstanding what 'real' means. For all the future tech and invented slang, this is a story about being yourself and following your passions regardless of some mainstream norm, that friendship isn't found in likes and retweets but in shared interests and caring for the well-being of someone other than yourself.

Other details and tics help bring unity to this collection. Names are repeated drawing potential links between seemingly unrelated character stories, no one has yet got round the problem of transposing them into a collection in a printed book. Here they are presented as a list, twenty-four covering three pages, encouraging you to read them from top to bottom rather than to treat each as a distinct piece. Each one blends into the next and the effect is underwhelming.

These two pieces feel like DVD extras, bonus material tagged on to the end and undermine the coherency of the whole.

That aside, *Invisible Planets* showcases Rajaniemi as one of the most imaginative and warm-hearted writers at work today. He never lets a neat idea get in the way of emotional truth and, as with great science fiction writers like John Wyndham, understands that fiction—all fiction, not just the science variety—is about exploring what it means to be a thinking, feeling, sentient being.

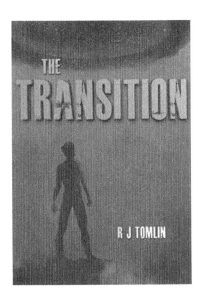

## The Transition
## R J Tomlin
## Self-published, 386 pages
## Review: Thom Day

*The Transition*, RJ Tomlin's most recent Young Adult offering, centres on Rume, an "elite" upperclassman in the Nethertower a week before he turns eighteen. The Nethertower houses hundreds or thousands (the book doesn't make it clear, and Rume isn't a very reliable narrator) of children aged between eleven and eighteen. Upon reaching their eighteenth birthdays, the elites undergo "the Transition" and join society outside. Before this, the kids work to meet their daily energy quota on VR-augmented exercise bikes. The Nethertower operates

like a capitalist training utopia: the kids are told that working hard will earn them credits for the outside world, and their work will mould them into the individuals they are destined to be. Trying to leave, communicate with the outside world, or failure to work are all strictly forbidden, and all elites must complete the Transition.

Rume is nervous in the lead-up to his Transition, and secretly keeps emails sent by his father. A final mysterious email leads to him attempting to escape the Nethertower with four of his friends on the eve of his Transition.

The rest of the book is an action-adventure as Rume and his friends try to discover what the Nethertower really is, who made it, and why. Along the way they fight off cannibals and zombies, meet new friends, and help the Resistance in their war against CARMA, all while Rume tries to figure out why his past seems inextricably tied to the fate of this new world.

The book is fast-paced and a real page-turner, the story ticks over with some tension. There are some genuinely enjoyable twists and surprises as well, which kept me wondering where the story would go next.

Unfortunately these weren't enough to cover the stilted dialogue and thinness of the landscape, and there were more than a few times I felt like giving up and putting the book aside. Rume seems to be experiencing the Nethertower for the first time along with the reader, rather than having grown up there. Baddies appear "out of nowhere" and the plot moved in one direction before abruptly veering off without explanation. The overall feeling is that this is an unfinished draft or a film treatment, rather than a completed novel. The characters come from the stock Young Adult Novel section and say the stock lines and do—for the most part— the stock things. The twists are very good and are the redeeming elements of the book, but they can't cover the plot holes, the cardboard landscapes, the unbelievable dialogue. The final reveal is inspired but ultimately disappointing, and left me with more questions than it provided satisfaction.

This is a young book by a young author; Tomlin is 21—barely older than Rume himself. He has four books under his belt already, and has just completed a one-man 100-day marketing campaign in Leeds city centre. He's passionate about writing and has strong reviews on Amazon. His enthusiasm shines through in *The Transition*; and while I may not be the first to pick up *The*

*Transition 2*, I do think Tomlin is one to watch.

## Behind The Throne
## K.B. Wagers
## 432 Pages
## Orbit Books
### Review: Benjamin Thomas

K.B. Wagers's debut science fiction novel *Behind the Throne*, the first in the Indranan War series, follows Hail Bristol, a runaway princess who has followed a much more dangerous career path: a notorious gunrunner. Tracked down twenty years after her crown-ditching escapade, Hail is brought back to the center of the Indranan Empire where her volatile relationship with her mother is mirrored by Indranan's relationship with its neighbours. With her siblings murdered and her mother ill, the rule of the Indranan Empire has been left in the hands of Hail's egotistical, conniving cousin.

Feeling alone and in the

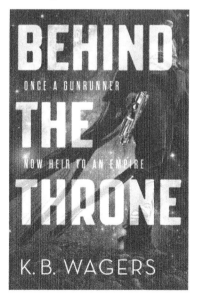

dead-centre of a place where she does not belong, Hail relies on her bodyguards Emmory and Zin, the same pair of Trackers that located her in deep space. With constant threats on her life, Hail must diplomatically shed her gunrunner behavior in favour for characteristics more suited for the heir to an empire. But she learns that changing who you really are is next to impossible.

What *Behind the Throne* does (aside from give us over four-hundred pages of fast-paced, badassness) is take situations that a good deal of people can relate to and set it against the epic back drop of a future matriarchal empire on the brink of war. This is what science fiction is supposed to do. It allows us to examine our own lives and the choices we make while being entertained by people from far off worlds.

While *Behind the Throne* does this, I was a little confused as to who exactly *us* was in this case. The novel is a fast-paced action romp with extremely well-written fight scenes, heavy language at times, and suggestions towards mature themes. However Hail is well into adulthood when she returns to the Indranan Empire and, unfortunately, doesn't always behave as such. I get what Wagers was attempting to do by making Hail have a difficult time adapting to life back home, but there was a very strong coming of age feel to every scene that involved Hail and her Empress mother. While I expected this to a degree, it was done so heavily that for a good chunk of the narrative I felt like I was reading a book geared towards a YA audience.

Muddled target audience aside, *Behind the Throne* was a very enjoyable read. It didn't bring anything shockingly new to the space epic sub-genre of science fiction, but it didn't need to. K.B. Wagers's pacing throughout the novel is by far one of my favourite things about it. It flows together flawlessly. The next novel in the series is due out mid-December and it's already on my Christmas list.

## Nod
**Adrian Barnes**
**Titan, 272 pages**
**Review: Noel Chidwick**

"All the old words are waking up and rubbing their eyes!"

Adrian Barnes has a slick way with words. His turns of phrase, his sharply focussed imagery means *Nod* is a treat to read.

The premise of Nod is fiendishly simple: Paul is a writer living in Vancouver. One morning he wakes up to find that no-one else slept; they literally did not sleep a wink. Quickly it becomes clear this is a world wide event, and Paul is one of only a handful of people who can sleep.

On day one people continue in a facsimile of normality, but after a second night of sleeplessness, the reality 'dawns' and Paul's world slowly dissolves. Two sides emerge, the 'Awakened' and the 'Sleepers', the Awakened are the majority, the living zombies. Paul's girlfriend, Tanya, can't sleep and she becomes jealous of Paul. It's clear early on that Paul needs to keep his normality hidden from those, who, after only a couple of days are suffering the hell of sleeplessness.

It's estimated that without sleep

you would certainly die within around four weeks: Paul's aim, in the end is to survive those four weeks.

Adrian Barnes forensically examines this new Vancouver and its people. The first, and last, response from the authorities is to implement the International Communication Ban, to "bring down the wall of static… and see if we could unclench our brains and snooze in the resulting stillness." The power is cut. The city has a few days of food stored on its shelves, then there is nothing. People are desperate to sleep, but can't. Paul and Tanya try to pick their way through this waking nightmare:

"Everybody I'd seen since leaving home looked like they were carrying an invisible case of nitro-glycerine in their shaking hands. Both dangerous *and* in danger"

Another layer of civilisation peels away, as Paul crushes the skull of an Awakened chasing a child Sleeper.

The question of whether a prophet, false or otherwise, would emerge from the chaos of dystopia every time is a theory we hope won't be tested, but we meet Charles, an Awakened who sees himself as a kind of prophet in this new world. Barnes raises the question of whether a prophet believes his own words, hides in them, or uses them as a way to keep himself alive and sane. But now it is too late; he has to keep talking.

We also meet Dave: clean-cut, organised and heading a quasi-military group who deny their sleeplessness. Their compound is hidden in the Dome of Science World. So normalised to the new world has Paul become when he

arrives there he asks Dave what he calls this place.

"'Science World, Paul. What are you on, man? It's called Science World. Quebec Street. Vancouver, British Columbia. Holy fuck, has everyone in the world gone crazy?'"

There's an acknowledgment of dystopian and post-apocalyptic fiction. *The Chrysalids, Animal Farm, Lord of the Flies, 1984*:

"Despairing visions. Every high school had taught these books. Every teen had been injected with them. What had possessed us?"

Throughout Nod, Barnes plays with language and words, and you can sense that he has to keep his lighter side in check for the sake of his story, for as Paul says:

"Humour had been the first casualty… and a humourless world seemed somehow even more tragic than one filled with pain and suffering."

Nod is an exhilarating and thoughtful novel.

WHERE ROCKETS BURN THROUGH

CONTEMPORARY SCIENCE FICTION POEMS FROM THE UK

Penned in *the Margins*

Edited by Russell Jones.

Blasting into the future, across alien worlds and distant galaxies, fantastic technologies and potential threats to humanity,

Where Rockets Burn Through brings science fiction and poetry together in one explosive, genre-busting collection.

Discover an array of poems by more than forty contemporary UK writers, including Edwin Morgan, Jane Yolen, Ron Butlin, WN Herbert, Ken MacLeod and Kirsten Irving, plus an exclusive essay on Sci-fi poetry by Steve Sneyd.

Preface by Alasdair Gray.

£9.99 paperback
Published by Penned in the Margins
www.pennedinthemargins.co.uk

# Multiverse

## Russell Jones

In this issue of Multiverse, the machines have taken over! Or, they've attempted to usurp humanity but couldn't climb our stairs. Tricksy stairs. These poems adopt humour as a way of discussing more philosophically complex and unnerving issues through the minds and mechanics of computers.

Andrew Blair's four-part poem, "Software User Agreement Update", blurs the lines between poem, dialogue, story and software protocol through its language and appearance on the page. It blends light and dark, humour with misery, isolation and insecurity, focussing on the mundane self-inflicted protocols of our own lives and relationships. Cheery.

Ruth Aylett's "Robophobia" also uses humour to explore the gaps between our expectations and reality, through the medium of robotics. "Unzip this plastic skin / search for ambition" the poem instructs us, as though our parts were removable. The poem explores whether we are able to expand beyond our physical and mental limitations, ending with the idea that our boundaries are what lead us to "climb different trees / to get us closer to the moon". Ruth's second poem, "Turing", takes a more serious look at issues such as logic, death and bigotry. It focusses on the work and life of Alan Turing, a ghost in all our machines, to discuss ideas of (im)permanence and mortality.

Far from the funtastic breakfast-making-machines and mishaps of 1980's comedy movies, on this evidence computers and robotics raise profound queries into what it means to be human in an ever-changing technological world. You'll never look at your iPhone in the same way again...

# Software User Agreement Update

### Section 1 - Our Relationship

Think of it as a friendship bracelet made from piano wire.
Think of it as Russia and the United States circa 1947 - 1991.
Think supply, supple, intransigent, skewed.

Want and ignorance.
Skimming and surface.

Power lies with the servants, gliding past the Arc of the Covenant to retrieve
what you have deemed necessary; we smother it til it lies still and despatch it
wearing - simultaneously - its death shroud and murder weapon.

We will accept blood as payment.
        Do not ask us what we do with it, we will not tell you.


### Section 2 - Your Rights

You're drowning in them, and that's fine, we respect that.
Once they are gone you will feel full of nothing, like a hunger without the
concept of food.

You will be phantom limbed,
A collapsed pier,
The truth about Santa,
The second last Russian Doll,
A closed mine.


### Section 3 - Just Scroll Past This Bit, Everyone Else Does

I may as well be the third person.

My job is to maintain these terms and conditions.

There are a surprising number of daily meetings.

Think of all the concepts that must thrive ethereal and fall into place, solid
and abstract, for this to be an occupation.

I ran after you because I thought I loved you. I'm sorry. I was eighteen and I'd
gluttonously consumed an idealised, battery farmed version of myself. I ran
after you because it could only be romantic. You weren't supposed to turn,

and slip, and break your shoulder, and take longer than expected to recover, and stop playing tournaments, and stop going to training, and stop trying. You were supposed to lift trophies, not work at the fish counter at Tesco. You were never meant to arrange trout into a fan pattern on a daily basis. You were never meant to be so precise, lining them up so their skin reflects colours you would never expect to see
in a fish.
You were never meant to take such pride in such work.
You were never meant to be happy like this.

I change the text in this section daily.

I've written 'Terms and Conditions apply' so often I've forgotten what it means.

## Section 4 - It's The End But The Moment Has Been Prepared For

Please tick this box.

Please tick it.

Any other form of symbol will be carved into my very living flesh and I will be dragged naked through the office while hooded figures chant 'Forbidden are these signs, forbidden are your joys'.

Our office has no cleaner.

Salt tears erase all traces of the unexpected.

Please tick this box if you do not wish to never unduly yet perhaps often nonetheless rigorously deny receiving a complete absence of content, love letters in the sand, a consenting genital, coordinates, names and a weapon; hats, a blow up doll with your face on it, breath down your back (lukewarm and sticky), iodine, the scent of hiding, postal meats, a list of everything you wanted to be, none of the above, plus the occasional Catfishing scam.

Please tick this box if you do not wish to know.

Please tick this box if you do not wish.

### *Andrew Blair*

---

**Andrew Blair** is a writer and performer based in Edinburgh, whose credits include *Gutter*, *Valve* and *Auld Enemies* project. He hosts the show *Poets Against Humanity*, and co-curates the *Lies, Dreaming* podcast.

---

# Robophobia

Genius solver of Sudoku,
chess grandmaster that
cannot pick up pieces,
arms that dent the wall
but fail to find the handle
on a cup, wheels that need
a nice flat floor,
turning for just two hours
until the battery's flat.

Unzip this plastic skin,
search for ambition
in the gears and motors.
You put a god in my machine, one
that chooses where the lightning
strikes, the cancer grows.
Make it a traveller from another village
where they do things wrong,
and therefore snatch
your history and friends
change your language, kill your songs.
Why scratch at that until it bleeds?

A simple ant, a slug
does better in the world
in getting food, producing ants
and slugs to carry on.
Oh, you argue, soon
you'll have all that and
then they'll be a threat.
Have you not seen
how we climb different trees
to get us closer to the moon?

*Ruth Aylett*

---

**Ruth Aylett** lives in Edinburgh where she teaches and researches university-level computing, thinks another world is possible and that the one we have is due some changes. She has been published by *New Writing Scotland, South Bank Poetry, Envoi, Bloodaxe Books, Poetry Scotland, Red Squirrel Press, Doire Press* and others. For more on her writing see: http://tinyurl.com/soi5e

# Turing

The ghost in this machine is his:
its processors
silicon flesh of his logic.

From here to there in steps.
He asked,
*Must you always*
*eventually arrive?*

Tracking those steps,
an impossible downward stair
looping into itself but
never reaching the ground.
The irresolvable resolves
into the logician who claims
he always lies.

He needed a machine;
made one in thought
that read, decided, wrote.
An unbounded tape
guiding, recording
steps chosen, steps carried out;
proved it was impossible
to be sure it would halt.

Read: a war and coded traffic
Write: decryption, a Bombe.
Read: body as machine
Write: machine intelligence.
Read: body as demand
Write: an opportunist young man.
Read: legalised bigotry
Write: chemical castration.

Read: an apple from
the tree of the knowledge of evil;
Write: space; and space; and space...

Where logic is not decidable
death is.

*Ruth Aylett*

# Parabolic Puzzles
## Paul Holmes

### Four Coloured Cubes

**After the Gravity train** delivered us to Gevassal, we made our way to the galaxy-famous Cubic Casino for a flutter.

We took our seats at the Asymmetric Table and the waitress brought us flaming Altarian cocktails. That—we all agreed—was Service! The croupier, Jade, explained the rules.

"It's an asymmetric dice game," said Jade. "You choose any dice and then I choose one, and we throw. The winner takes the stakes. If it's a draw, we roll again. Simple."

She handed the dice to me and said "But you'd better inspect them first." "What unusual dice!" I observed. "The yellow sides add up to 22 and the green add up to 24, but I suspect the yellow would beat the green more often than not. Hmm!"

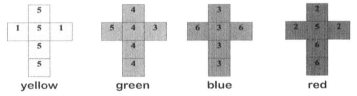

| yellow | green | blue | red |

I picked up the blue dice, as this also added to 24 and I reckoned this would give me the best chance of winning.

Which dice did Jade pick up?

A while later I decided to take my chances with a different dice. "May I change colours?" I asked.

"Certainly," replied Jade, "Which one would you like?"

"I think I'll try the Green this time."

"Here you are," she said with a twinkling smile.

Which dice did Jade pick up this time?

***Send your answer to us via our website Contact Form. If you are correct, your name will be dropped into a hat. A copy of Duncan Lunan's book* The Elements of Time *will be sent to the lucky name pulled out of said hat.***

Puzzles by **Paul Holmes** is published by The New Curiosity Shop and is available from bookshops or online. Paul's next collection, *The Galactic Festival* will be published by Shoreline of Infinity Publications in late 2016.

Lightning Source UK Ltd.
Milton Keynes UK
UKOW06f0029160916

283120UK00001B/37/P